BERLIN
CENTRE

ALSO BY MAX HERTZBERG

The East Berlin Series
Stealing The Future (2015)
Thoughts Are Free (2016)
Spectre At The Feast (2017)

Reim Series
Stasi Vice (2018)
Operation Oskar (2019)
Berlin Centre (2019)

Other Fiction
Cold Island: A Brexit Novel (2018)

Non-fiction
with Seeds For Change
How To Set Up A Workers' Co-op (2012)
A Consensus Handbook (2013)

After the experience of the East German political upheaval in 1989/90 Max Hertzberg became a Stasi files researcher. Since then he has also been a book seller and a social change trainer and facilitator.
Visit the author's website for background information on the GDR, and guides to walking tours around the East Berlin in which many of his books are set.

www.maxhertzberg.co.uk

Berlin Centre

Max Hertzberg

P 1 2 3 4 5 6 7 8 9 10

Published in 2019 by Max Hertzberg
www.maxhertzberg.co.uk

Copyright ©Max Hertzberg 2019.

Max Hertzberg has asserted his right under the Copyright, Designs
and Patents Act 1988 to be identified as the author of this work.

Cover photograph copyright ©Michel Huhardeaux, licensed under the
Creative Commons Attribution 2.0 International Licence.

Text licensed under the Creative Commons Attribution-Non-
Commercial-No-Derivatives 4.0 International License. View a copy
of this license at: www.creativecommons.org/licenses/by-nc-nd/4.0/

c/o Wolf Press, 22 Hartley Crescent, LS6 2LL

A CIP record for this title is available from the British Library
ISBN: 9781913125028 (paperback), 9781913125028 (large print paperback),
9781913125035 (epub)

Set in 10½ on 12pt Linux Libertine O

All characters in this publication, except for those named public figures who
are used in fictional situations, are fictitious and any resemblance to real
persons, living or dead, is entirely unintended and coincidental.

DECEMBER 1983

1
BERLIN LICHTENBERG

My old pal Holger walked into my new office early on a Thursday morning.

"You've had a promotion," I told him after counting the pips on his shoulder.

"Change of scenery, too," he replied, twisting his head so he could join in with the counting. "Been transferred to HA II."

Small talk exhausted, I told him to shut the door while I got the bottle and glasses out. He was my first visitor at Berlin Centre, and that called for a toast.

"You know that favour you owe me," he asked once he'd emptied his glass.

I knew I owed him a favour, I just didn't know which one he was referring to. But he was probably here to let me know, so I topped up his glass and settled back, ready to hear what Holger had to offer.

"Practically the first job across my desk," he said, sipping his vodka. "I've been assigned to look after a walk-in, would you believe?"

"Congratulations," I replied. I'd never had a *Selbstanbieter*, a member of a foreign security service walk up to me and offer their services as an informant.

"They sent me to pick him up from Beeskow. Let's call him Subject Bruno, that's what his file says after all. Bruno from Bonn. He's visiting relatives over here and decides to make himself known to the local county office—they're all in a swither and phone Berlin. Berlin phones me and tells me to go and get him."

I took a sip of vodka. What Holger was saying sounded interesting, better than pushing the same piece of paper round my desk all day, which was what I'd been doing ever since I got here.

I topped up our glasses and waited for him to get to the point.

"So I drove out to Beeskow—you know the place?"

I knew it. I'd passed through on the motorcycle once or twice. One of those sandpit towns that lurk in the endless Prussian forests of Brandenburg.

"Picked him up, brought him back," continued Holger. "On the way, we got chatting, hit it off a bit. He was easy to talk to."

I could already tell I wasn't going to like where this was going.

"He's had a week of the treatment and now they're going through the transcripts, deciding what to do with him. While that's happening, he's to behave himself and sit tight.

"So, yesterday I took him to a *Datschek* in the woods. Nice joint, they're keeping him sweet: good food, more than enough beer and a couple of guards to split firewood and feed the stove when he's feeling cold. I reckon the plan is to make sure he arrives back in Bonn on time so they can play him back to the opposition. Of course, there's a hair in the soup." Holger paused to light a cigarette. I let him get on with it, I was enjoying story hour. "There's always a hair in the soup and this time it's the source himself. It seems our new friend Bruno from Bonn is getting bored." Holger paused to take another sip of vodka, watching me over the rim of his glass.

"You want me to feel sorry for him?"

"Wait, listen—this is the best bit: I had to take some paperwork down there this morning, had a bit of a chat with Bruno. He told me he's frustrated that the one good bit of intelligence he brought with him hasn't been acted upon."

"How's he know what we're doing with intelligence he

provided?" I snorted, this was obvious stuff, even to a walk-in *Westler*.

"Exactly. Normally he wouldn't know. Except this time he does because when I picked him up from Berlin, during a nice chat on the way to the *Datschek*—he told me about a mole in the Firm."

That made me sit up straight. Moles are bad news for everyone, and speaking personally, the last thing I needed was a deep probe tunnelling through the whole Ministry, I had too much smelly laundry that wasn't fit for the light of day.

"Wait, it gets even better." Holger held his glass out for another top-up. "One of the officers who interrogated him— Bruno from Bonn says the interrogator is the mole."

2
BERLIN LICHTENBERG

It doesn't do to wander around Berlin Centre saying such things.

The first thing I did was double check my office door was closed. The next thing I did was pull an army blanket out of the bottom drawer of the filing cabinet and put the telephone to bed, tucking it tight in the grey blanket.

"A mole? You sure he wasn't just trying to cause trouble?" I asked.

"Always a possibility."

"You passed on the information?"

"Wrote the report, never got round to handing it in—you know what happens to messengers."

We looked at each other for a while, sipping our vodka. I wasn't enjoying the conversation and needed Holger out of my office. But he wanted something from me, and he wouldn't go until he'd asked. I gave him his line: "What do you want?"

"If I hand that report in—it's about members of my department and I've only just arrived. Doesn't do to make allegations like that, not without collateral."

"I'm not the one to-" I had my hands up in front of me, shaking my head.

But Holger wasn't in a listening mood. "Just have a wee poke around, see if there's anything to it. If it looks like Bruno's telling the truth then I'll hand in my report. Start my new posting with a bang—breaking something like this would set me on the right path."

"It'll also make you lots of enemies. Particularly if anyone finds out about it before you get that collateral you were just talking about."

"That's why I'm asking for help." Holger's face was a picture of innocence.

"Listen, pal, I've only just got here myself. Haven't even got my feet under the table yet. What you're asking ... something like this, I'd have to take it to the section chief."

"Be a good start for you. You run it, I'll help out any way I can. That way we'll both get some credit."

Holger had a point, and I liked the way he said it. He could have got on his high horse, gone on about all he's done for me over the years, how much I owe him. But he didn't do that, he just offered me half the glory.

And all the risk.

3
BERLIN LICHTENBERG

When my last posting ended, I'd decided I was ready for the quiet life. I'd put in for a transfer to Neubrandenburg district headquarters—nothing much happens up there, and there's nothing to do but watch the trees grow. No borders to the West, so no need to worry about escapees. The district does touch Poland, and to be fair, the way the Poles have been behaving the last few years, that border might become a problem yet.

I packed my bags and sat on them, waiting for my transfer to the empty north, but it never came. Instead, they assigned me to ZAIG, the Ministry's Central Evaluation and Information Group, based at Berlin Centre in Lichtenberg.

On the first day, they gave me an office, complete with desk, typewriter and telephone, and told me to wait for further orders. Then they forgot all about me.

The first person to come near had been Holger, and he'd left again as soon as he'd told me what he wanted me to do. So I was back to me, myself and I in a poky office, gawping at a telephone wrapped in an army blanket.

I released the phone, folded and stowed the coarse, grey wool, all the while thinking about the time bomb Holger had brought.

If he was right about there being a mole in the Ministry then sooner or later the wolves would be unleashed, and they'd shred every secret from every body they came across, quick or dead. After the last two cases I'd worked, I couldn't afford that level of scrutiny—I didn't even know whether I was still in the frame for the death of my old Boss, Major Fröhlich. Nor did I know whether the disappearance of my wife had gone unremarked, or whether they just hadn't got round to interrogating me yet.

I was still hoping nobody knew about my involvement in Operation Oskar and the disappearance of Major Blecher—but when it comes to the Firm, there's no telling. Wily bastards can watch you for years, perfecting their plans. Until they decide the time is right, you'll be none the wiser.

Perhaps Holger was right. Help him defuse the time bomb and we'd both get gold stars. And gold stars, when attached to shoulder boards, mean more salary and more privileges.

Holger's story interested me. I hadn't taken any notes, it was all in my head and I rattled through the little information he'd given me.

What it boiled down to was the word of a walk-in—someone prepared to betray his own country and his own colleagues. A discontented officer of the BKA, the West German Federal Crime Agency, tired of working on the rolling-up of the second generation of the terrorist Red Army Fraction. Even if his job involved assessing intelligence on the GDR's involvement in supporting the RAF, I couldn't see how he'd get hold of information about a mole in our department.

Source Bruno's story didn't ring true. His word wasn't good enough to justify releasing the wolves on Berlin Centre.

4
BERLIN LICHTENBERG

It was nearly a week before I next saw Holger. I'd been to his office in the next building along, but the secretary had sent me on my way again. Quoting the paranoid security regulations of the Ministry, she refused to tell me when he might be back. The decrepit aunt wouldn't even take a message.

So I went back to my own office and continued to wait for someone to notice that I existed.

And my existence was duly noted at the Party branch meeting the next morning when I was taken in hand by the Party deputy-secretary who gave me a pile of membership files to tidy.

Years of training, years of operational experience, and I end up in a tiny office, wondering how Comrade *Unteroffizier* Rietig's Party records had ended up in Comrade *Gefreiter* Reicherl's file.

I clocked off late that day, same as every other day. When a superior officer comes knocking on my door, holding the files for a challenging and interesting operation, I want to be there, showing a keen face.

Which is why it was after 2000 hours when I left. Ignoring the steps down to the U-Bahn, I turned right and started the walk home. A bit of exercise would do me good after sitting behind the desk, drinking schnapps and smoking all day.

It was winter, in fact it was nearly Christmas—the lights from the shop windows flared festively on the damp pavements—but since the weekend the weather had turned mild. Temperatures were well above freezing, the snow and ice had melted, and puddles lay on the buckled paving stones. I loosened my coat, pulled my thick mittens off and admired how my hands glowed in the damp air.

I went past the bar outside Frankfurter Allee S-Bahn station, it was out of bounds to Ministry personnel, nevertheless the idea of an anonymous beer in a fusty *Kneipe* appealed. More appealing than sitting at home by myself, watching television.

Despite the lure of the various bars I passed, I made it to the far end of Friedrichshain without being led astray. It seemed simpler to count my miseries in the comfort of my own home.

As I turned the final corner, I could see the streetlamps on my side of the road still hadn't been repaired, one or two glimmered outside the old-build tenements opposite, but the concrete walkway to my front door was in darkness.

Trusting my winter boots not to soak up the puddles, I stomped through meltwater to my block door and let myself in. I didn't check to see if there was any post, I didn't bother to read the new notices from the municipal accommodation administration, just headed straight upstairs to my own flat.

I opened the front door and went in, taking off my coat and boots while doing a mental stocktake of fridge and cupboards. There'd be some of that crispbread I hated, but other than that, who knew? I turned around, deciding I needed to go into the kitchen to see whether I had anything edible, but I only got as far as the living room.

"*Verdammt nochmal,*" I swore under my breath.

Holger was sitting in my favourite armchair, holding a bottle of my beer and looking serious.

"This is not funny," I told him.

"We need to talk."

I swiped my hand through the air, brushing him off, and headed to the fridge for a beer.

"What's wrong with looking me up at work?" I asked once

I'd got settled on the sofa.

"I've been away."

"I had noticed." It wasn't just his absence from the Centre that I'd noted, it was the Lufthansa bag at his feet, and the creased Western suit he was wearing.

But I left the conversation where it had run aground. Sipped my beer and waited for Holger to tell me why he'd broken into my flat. Whatever his reasons, they would have to be good—over the last few months, too many people had seen my front door as an open invitation, and the heavy traffic was giving me dyspepsia.

Holger finished his beer and got up to fetch a new one. "Need another?" he asked as he went past.

"Kind of you to offer."

"No problem, it's your beer anyway." Holger didn't recognise sarcasm.

He opened a couple of bottles and handed me one on his way back to my armchair.

"I needed that." He opened his mouth wide for a burp, then polished his gob with the back of his hand. "You're probably wondering why I was waiting for you?"

"You were waiting for me? I assumed you'd just run out of beer."

"I've been to Bonn."

"Not good for your health this time of year—heard it's a little damp."

"Reim—shut up and let me get a word in edgeways. I was babysitting Bruno, making sure he got home OK. Usual drill: house him, bed him in, confirm channels of communication-"

"Was?" He might have told me to shut up but I'm not a secret policeman for nothing, I'd picked up on the way he'd emphasised the past tense.

"Bruno was arrested on Saturday. They were waiting for him at his flat in Meckenheim, grabbed him as soon as he got home."

10

"So, they found out he'd had a chat with us. Stands to reason," I ventured. "Look on the bright side, at least you got away."

But Holger was shaking his head. "No. Everything was going exactly to plan: he took the train he was booked on, arrived home the right day, the right time. Everything as expected, there was no reason for any suspicions."

"You say this happened on Saturday? Where have you been since?"

"Dortmund. Never thought I'd end up in a safe house in Dortmund, but that's where they put me. Two days of debriefing, they let me come back this afternoon." Holger took a pull of his beer, then another. "I came straight here, but they'll have more questions for me at the Centre tomorrow."

I gave my friend a closer look, noting the dark bags under his eyes, the heavy eyelids. The hand holding the bottle was trembling.

I made a trip to the kitchen and came back with a couple of glasses and a bottle of *Doppelkorn*. Holger downed his in one go, so I filled him up again.

"OK, Holger, let's hear it from the top, nice and slow—we've got the whole evening ahead of us."

Holger took it from the top. From when he collected Source Bruno from the county administration in Beeskow, to the moment he watched Bruno being bundled into the back of a black Mercedes in a small West German town on the outskirts of Bonn.

All the usual counter-surveillance measures had been put in place while Bruno was still on the territory of the GDR. As soon as he'd made contact with the local operative in Beeskow, he'd been mothered—even if there had been a Western minder out there trying to keep tabs on Bruno, the chances of the defector being spotted while talking to us were as close to zero as the Firm could manage. And in this Republic, that was damn close.

No, the West Germans must have had another reason to nick the source.

Listening to my friend talk, it was clear he thought he knew the answer to the riddle.

"You know how it is, the most likely scenario is the one that's probably true," he told me. "Time and again we see it. Why go hunting for far-out explanations? We're not a regiment of Miss Marples; we deal in facts, not fiction. And the most obvious explanation in this case-"

"Don't say it!" I leant forward, elbows on my knees, looking into Holger's eyes. But there was no stopping him.

"That mole Bruno talked about. It was the mole that told the West Germans about Bruno's defection."

I couldn't disagree with Holger, in our game we concentrate on the most likely explanations first. But he and I differed in our opinions on what the most likely reason for Source Bruno's arrest might be. Right now, I wasn't prepared to commit to any theory, not until I'd found out a bit more.

I didn't think I'd get much sense out of Holger tonight and tried to send him home. Trouble was, he refused to leave.

"What about your family?" I coaxed.

"They don't know I'm back yet," he replied, burying his head in his hands.

It wasn't just that he was tired from the nursemaid operation and the subsequent debriefing, he was in a funk. He'd already been vigorously debriefed and was expecting more of the treatment when he reported for duty in the morning. He'd failed in a simple babysitting mission and he knew the Centre would be looking to spread the blame on his bread.

I took the bed and gave Holger the sofa. I'm not heartless, he got a blanket too. And I even doled out a few sleeping pills of my wife's that were cluttering up the bathroom cabinet.

★

In the morning I woke up in as good a mood as can be expected in mid-December, but Holger looked no better for his few hours on the couch.

"We can go to work separately, I don't want to drag you down with me ..." he mumbled around the edge of his coffee.

I slapped him on the shoulder and told him to cheer up, but he wasn't having any of it. He left the flat and his half-full cup of coffee, and I sat at the table a while longer.

He wasn't wrong about dragging others down with him. I would be avoiding Holger as much as I could.

5
BERLIN LICHTENBERG

I next saw Holger a couple of days later. It was midday, I was in the canteen, eating *Kohlroulade*. Or, to put it more accurately, I was scraping congealed sauce off the soapy cabbage when I saw him at the serving counter. I left my half-eaten lunch where it was and took the side door.

Did I feel guilty about avoiding my friend? No, he'd have done the same. In fact, just a few weeks ago I was the one who had been bad news and Holger had gone to great lengths to avoid being seen in my company. He knew where to find me if he wanted a chat.

Back behind my empty desk—the Party membership files had all been checked and returned—I couldn't help but mull over Holger's predicament. Or rather, Bruno's.

Eventually, Holger would be pronounced Persil clean, or maybe he wouldn't. I had no influence over the process, it was all down to his department.

But, just for the sake of keeping our brains active, let's take Source Bruno's assertion at face value. Let's assume for the moment that he was right about the mole in Main Department II—that would not only account for Bruno's arrest in West Germany, it would also explain why they were giving Holger such a hard time now he was home. It would be in the mole's interest to ensure Bruno was removed from the scene and that Holger would then take the fall for betraying the source.

Still not convinced? Me neither, which is why I began to list other scenarios.

Perhaps Bruno had been arrested for something he'd said or

14

done before he came to visit his relatives over here—the timing of his arrest a mere coincidence. I grunted as the C word crossed my mind—it seemed every detective novel ever published and every episode of *Polizeiruf 110* on the telly made some comment about never trusting coincidences. But I live in the real world, not between the blue covers of a *Krimi* published by *Delikte Indizien Ermittlungen*. And in the real world, coincidences happen.

I knew nothing about Bruno. I had no way of knowing whether he was involved in criminal activities in the West, or even whether he'd let slip some clue that he was planning to defect. The possibilities were endless.

Poor Holger, caught up in this mess. I hoped the brass would realise he wasn't to blame for Bruno's arrest, and hoping was the best I could do for him.

And what about Bruno's mole? As far as I was concerned: case closed.

My office phone rang for the first time that afternoon. I stared at the receiver as it vibrated its way through each long ding of the bell. Whoever had dialled wasn't going away.

"*Unterleutnant* Reim," I answered after the fourth ring.

"Comrade Second Lieutenant, report immediately to Comrade Major Kühn's office."

I was on my feet, standing at attention. It was that kind of voice. But it didn't wait for any response from me, it had already rung off.

I straightened the creases on my trousers, ran a rag over my shiny shoes and rolled my shoulders and shot my cuffs until I was satisfied my uniform jacket was sitting correctly. This was it, I was finally going to be given a task.

Major Kühn had his office on a plush corridor with all the other *Bonzen* in ZAIG. He was deputy of the second section—control and measurement. In good German that simply means keeping an eye on all the other Ministry employees.

I marched into the office, clickety-heeled in front of the bulky, balding officer behind the desk. Wider than he was high, heavy brow folded over the same kind of thick-rimmed glasses worn by Comrade General Secretary Honecker.

Major Kühn, if that's who it was behind the desk, did what all superior officers like to do when first meeting a subordinate. He ignored me.

I remained at attention, staring through the inevitable portrait of General Mielke that was interrupting the pattern on the wallpaper. The major himself continued to examine an advert in a Western newspaper, grainy pictures of sausages and cuts of meat with the smudged yellow and red logo of a cheap supermarket in the corner.

I can't swear to it—I was too busy being polite and staring at the wall—but I'm pretty certain I could hear him lick his lips.

The newspaper rustled and the major spoke for the first time.

"Comrade Second Lieutenant Heym," he began, still smacking his lips. I knew better than to correct him. "From your records I see you're an experienced analyst, so I'm going to try you out in that field. There's an operational process I want you to look at, see where it went wrong. Who messed up, what lessons are to be learnt. Think you can handle that?"

I kept my eyes on the wallpaper and my thumbs aligned with my trouser seams. No reply required.

"Report directly to me. The files are on the table behind you, paper research only at this stage."

A rustle of newspaper told me I'd been dismissed. A *Jawohl, Genosse Major*, more clickety-heels, about turn and with a neat sweep of my arm as I went past, I caught the low stack of files from the table.

"We need a quick turn-around on this. Interim report by tomorrow afternoon, Comrade *Unterleutnant*," the major called after me, meaning I had to about turn and repeat the whole tap of the heels shebang and all that goes with it.

I managed to get out of the office without doing any more impressions of a typewriter and, returning along the corridor, I relaxed my shoulders and my gait and took a gander at the files I'd been given.

The top one was a cadre file, the name on the front meant nothing to me. I slid that to one side and looked at the next one down, then the one after: names of personnel I didn't know, hadn't met and had never heard of.

I shoved the files under my arm and carried on towards my office, looking forward to the job ahead of me. Kühn had made clear this was a paper exercise only, but with a bit of luck he might let me interrogate the people whose names were on the covers of these files. I'd tell him it was important to keep my hand in.

Back at my office, I shut the door, fanned the folders out on the desk and took a closer look.

None of the names on the first few files rang any bells, couldn't even tell you what department they belonged to or even whether they were based in Berlin or in the provinces. I shuffled through a few more, all unknown. Until the last but one. Here was a name I recognised.

Holger Fritsch

I sat for a while, looking at the writing on the front of the folder. Holger my old pal. Holger, the one who was currently contagious. Holger whose file was on my desk. I pushed it to one side, revealing the cover of the final folder. This wasn't a cadre file, it was an asset file, and the name on the front came as no surprise.

There was a stamp showing a date from last week, below that, neatly written in blue ink along a dotted line:

Source Bruno

6
BERLIN LICHTENBERG

I pushed all but the last two files aside and stared at the covers. To the left I had Holger, to my right was Bruno.

I shouldn't even open these files. I should march straight back to Major Kühn and tell him I couldn't take the case. Or I could take a quick look first—might find something useful in there for Holger.

I dithered for a minute, then opened up the file. I didn't have to tell my superior that I knew Holger—if anyone asked, I'd report the fact that we'd been at the Ministry's high school in Golm together, tell them we had never even worked in the same building since then. We just knew each other to nod to in the corridor, to share small talk over a coffee in the canteen.

Hardly knew each other at all. No conflict of interest.

After leafing through Holger's file and not seeing anything that seemed relevant to the case, I turned to Source Bruno, real name Arnold Seiffert, date of birth 27th of February 1952.

It was all there, for each visit there was the usual collation of data: photostat of his West German identity card, copies of the visa authorisation, the visa itself along with the customs declaration, registration and deregistration forms from the local police station, receipt for compulsory currency exchange. The dates of his last trip matched those Holger had told me.

So far, so boring.

A report by the ABV, the local beat officer, was next. Source Bruno's relatives, who lived in a village a few kilometres from Beeskow, were nondescript. An aunt and an uncle, she was a baker's assistant, retired, he was a machinist at a collective farm, also retired. Other than membership in the trade union and the Society for German-Soviet Friendship, neither were politically organised. A quiet couple who hadn't come to the attention of the beat officer.

There's nothing like a stack of dry files to make you thirsty. I thought about the bottle in the bottom drawer of the desk, but decided against. I wanted to stay sharp.

Wasn't Bruno subject to restrictions by his employers? Could BKA officials just travel to East Germany whenever they felt like it? Or did they need some kind of permission?

I wrote the questions in my notebook and returned to reading about Bruno's relatives—despite having never met them or Bruno, I was beginning to hate them purely on the basis of these tedious reports. In fact, it was all so boringly normal that I felt I must have missed something and went back to the start. It was just as slow and stale on the second reading.

Bruno's parents left East Germany in 1950, just over a year before he was born. They passed through Berlin and settled near Osnabrück, in the north-west of West Germany. Both had become civil servants: the father a postman, the mother a schoolteacher. Just like their relatives who stayed over here, there was no record of political activity.

I leaned back in my chair and stared at the wall opposite, trying to keep my mind away from the schnapps. This was slow, dull work, and it would get worse before it got better— I'd have to see whether Bruno's relatives had their own files that could shed light on his background, anything that might explain his interest in working for us.

I put the parents to one side and returned to the background report on Bruno himself. For someone who came to the GDR so regularly, and a BKA officer at that, the report seemed a little slim. It held little information beyond what could be read on his visa application form: date of birth

(27.02.1952), marital status (single), dates of entry to GDR (four, at intervals of between two and three years, twice arriving by train, twice by vehicle), occupation (Federal Crime Agency official) and on it went. There was nothing even vaguely useful here.

I stared at the wallpaper, my eyes tracing the faint green pattern over the buff background, then with a sigh I closed the folder and placed it, along with the other files in the steel cupboard, sealing the doors before leaving my office.

In the canteen I sipped a weak coffee and nibbled a dry pastry. The place was nearly empty, just me and the serving staff. Clangour and shouts came from the kitchen area as supper was prepared for those officers who were working late.

Bruno was West German-born, I summarised the day's reading to myself, still feeling I'd missed something. Regular visits to his mother's sister and her husband, dating back to when he'd finished his national service.

His parents, on the other hand, had never returned—not surprising considering they'd left the GDR illegally and would be worried about being arrested if they came back. But what about the aunt and uncle? They were retired, which meant they were free to apply for visas for travel to the West, yet the aunt had never shown any interest in visiting her sister in Osnabrück.

Correspondence between the two sisters was sparse: Christmas greetings, a letter for birthdays, and not even that every year. But Bruno regularly wrote to his aunt and uncle, sent parcels of coffee, clothes and chocolate. Interesting family dynamics going on there—I wondered why it was that Bruno was showing more interest in maintaining family ties than his mother did.

Were Bruno's visits to his aunt and uncle merely cover to enter the GDR?

7
BERLIN LICHTENBERG

Back from the canteen, I picked up Bruno's file and flipped past the personal details until I got to the reports of his defection and debriefing.

I read through the accounts without pause, just to get a feel of it, building a mental picture of what had happened. By the time I finished it was getting dark.

I leaned back in my chair, eyes smarting, and reached down to get the bottle. I rewarded my efforts with one drink, then switched the light on and began reading again.

Files are never exactly exciting, but it's hard not to get frustrated when the juicy bits have been redacted. There was no finesse about it, just a gap in the dates where pages had been removed—everything and anything from the moment Holger picked up Bruno in Beeskow until the morning Bruno left the safe house named Building 74 to catch the train to Cologne. Nine days' worth of files, covering the interrogation of Bruno and his preparation as an informant and agent of the Ministry.

I packed the files into the safe and sealed them in, then picked up my coat and bag and left the office.

A Siberian wind whipped the fine rain and gusted through the courtyards of Berlin Centre, I kept tight hold of my ID card as I showed it to the sentry on the side gate on my way out, worried it would be blown from my grasp.

On exiting, I tucked the clapperboard away, I hunched my way down Magdalenenstrasse, one hand pressed to my hat, keeping it safe on my head, the other clutching my briefcase.

This wasn't a night for walking home, perhaps it wasn't a night for going home at all—instead of diving down the steps into the warmth of the U-Bahn station, I struggled along Frankfurter Allee as far as the tram stop. The wind hissed past me down the boulevard, pushing me along, old newspapers and leaves overtook me.

I caught the number three tram, and sat at the back, all the better to observe boarding passengers. It was an old habit, but tonight I had a minor justification for taking care. I wanted to ask Holger a few questions, and it was probably best if no-one saw me do it.

The tram rocked along Ho-Chi-Minh-Strasse, buffeted by the storm as it gusted through the wide junctions, and I had to hold tight as I made my way to the doors to get off at the Dynamo Sportforum. I stopped a schoolkid who was hauling a handcart full of soggy newspapers into the rain.

"I'll give you fifty Pfennigs to take a message."

The kid stood bandy-legged on the slick pavement, keeping tight hold of his little wagon. He looked me up and down and thought about the offer.

"I'm on my way to the recycling shop." He thought about it a bit more. "And there's a bad weather surcharge today," he had to shout over the traffic and the whistling trees.

"Fifty Pfennigs from me now and another fifty from the comrade I'm sending you to see. Deal?"

I gave the brat Holger's address and told him to pass on the message that a comrade wanted to see him at the tram stop.

"A comrade wants to see you?" asked the boy. "Is that all?"

While I was waiting for Holger to turn up, I stood in a phone box. I was out of the wind in there, it was dry, and I could keep an eye on my surroundings through the glass. Mouthing random phrases into a dead receiver, I watched the queue of cars shuffle towards the petrol station next door.

Holger had the nous not to join me in the telephone box, he shoved his hands into the pockets of his raincoat and joined the queue at the tram stop, his gaze set on the road.

As the tram rumbled up, Holger shifted slightly, glancing at me from the corner of his eye. I nodded, hung up and left the phone box, sprinting towards the tram as Holger boarded.

I sprang up the steps as the bell rang to warn of the doors closing and sank into a seat a few rows in front of Holger. Neither of us acknowledged each other, we just sat there, buried in the collars of our coats while the tram ground through the tight streets of Weissensee.

I got off three stops later, aware that Holger had followed me. From the vague reflections in the darkened shop windows we passed, I could see that it was just the two of us on the side road. I turned a corner and waited for Holger to catch up.

"Reim," he said as he shook my hand. "Shit weather."

The weather wasn't so bad up here, the streets were narrower so the wind didn't have much chance to pick up so much momentum. But it was still raining. More than enough reason to visit the pub on the next corner.

Low-wattage bulbs did their best to cast thin light on the dark surfaces of solid-wood tables that had survived the war. The bar was varnished to a shade of brown that was almost black and the beer was thin and warm. The landlord looked like he was as old as the tables, the backs of his hands were covered in age-spots that were the same colour as his bar.

I signalled for another two beers as we sat down near the back, as far as possible from the bar and its only patron, a veteran wearing a worker's denim jacket, a flannel check shirt and braces.

"They've asked me to go over Bruno files," I told Holger as I lit two cigarettes and gave him one.

The top-ups were already on their way, the old man's hands shaking as he placed the glasses on the table, spilling beer as he did so.

"Did you tell them you know me?" Holger asked once the old man had shuffled back to his perch behind the bar.

"Curiosity's a dangerous thing," I replied. "Thought I'd save them from that particular sin. They want me to work out who they can blame for what happened in Bonn."

My friend's shoulders slumped when he heard that. He must have known it would be this way, had probably drafted his self-criticism speech, ready for when they asked him to fall on his sword.

"That's the bad news," I said after I'd had some beer. "The good news is that there's nothing in the files to suggest any of it was your fault."

"I was the last person to see the source, I was with him all the way from Königs Wusterhausen to Bonn. They're going to say it was me, of course they are!"

"Have some beer, Holger. It's not as bad as you think, not yet. Like I said, there's nothing in the files ..." I watched Holger start his second glass. His hands were shaking as much as the landlord's. "Listen, they've given me the reports for when you picked up Bruno, and the reports of his journey from the safe house to when he was arrested in Meckenheim. But everything in between those two events is missing. I can't make an assessment when the important bits are missing."

"And that's what you'll tell them, that you can't put the blame on anyone?"

"That's what I'll tell them," I reassured him.

I finished my second beer and watched Holger stare into his half-full glass. He wasn't much of a drinker tonight.

"So you'll ask to interview the other operatives who were in contact with him? The drivers, and the guards at the safe house near Briesen? I can probably find out who they were, shouldn't be a problem-"

"No need for that just yet." I did a slow-down motion with my hands, the last thing we needed was for Holger to go barging about, asking for names. "But since we're on the subject—you said Bruno thought one of his interrogators was a mole. Any idea which one he meant?"

Holger was staring into his beer again, arms crossed in front of him. He shook his head.

"No clues? Did Bruno refer to them as he, or she? Did he have much contact with the mole?"

Holger was still shaking his head. "But if I find out the names—the babysitters and other personnel—you'd talk to them, you'd do that for an old friend, wouldn't you?"

"Yes," I told him as I signalled for another beer.

But that was a lie. After the last case I'd decided I was going to do everything by the book. No freelance enquiries, no poking my nose in matters that didn't concern me. Not without orders.

Not even for an old friend.

8
BERLIN LICHTENBERG

I didn't tell Holger that I already knew the names of the other babysitters who had looked after Bruno, nor that I already had their cadre files. Nevertheless, he had a point: I wouldn't find out what had really happened by reading written reports. To do the job properly I needed to talk to everyone involved.

But Major Kühn didn't agree. He'd have his reasons for only giving me half the reports and half the names, and my job was to look at the files and type up a report. If he wanted me to do more than that, he'd have to give me more access.

I spent the morning typing and retyping the report, managing to get it to Kühn's secretary just before she went to lunch.

"This isn't due until this afternoon," she informed me, her voice colder than last night's wind.

"Then give it to the Comrade Major this afternoon," I replied as I walked out of her office.

Back behind my own desk, I sat and stared at the telephone. I knew it would ring before too long.

In the end, it took a while longer than expected, and the whole time I was waiting, staring at the phone, I was mentally preparing myself for what would come.

"Second Lieutenant Reim," I said into the mouthpiece when, thirty-seven minutes later, the phone finally rang.

"Comrade Major Kühn's office. Now." It was the secretary, and she clearly wasn't in a talkative mood, since she hung up before I could reply.

★

26

"What is the meaning of this?" demanded Kühn when I toddled into his office. He had my report in front of him, just one side of A4, less if you ignored the file numbers, dates, personal codes and all the other obligatory bureaucratic garnishes.

I didn't answer, the major would let me know when he wanted an answer.

"I asked for operational analysis, not this, this ..." he waved my report at me as if worried I wouldn't know what he was talking about. "*No conclusions can be drawn from the currently available material ...*" he stopped waving the piece of paper long enough to read his favourite bit.

I had my eyes glued to the wall above his head so I couldn't tell you what his face was doing during all of this. It probably wasn't very pretty anyway.

"Well, Heym—what have you got to say for yourself? Don't just stand there like a sausage-monger!"

Under different circumstances I might have enjoyed his sense of humour.

"Comrade Major Kühn, permission to speak?" I was still standing at attention, thumbs along trouser seams, chest puffed out until the buttons down the front of my jacket were armed and ready to fire, shoulders back far enough for the secretary to see the pips on my epaulettes.

On the edge of my vision, I saw the major wave his hand. That was my permission.

"Comrade Major Kühn, after detailed analysis of the reports made available to me, I came to the conclusion that there were no operative or operatives, whether acting singly or jointly, engaged in any act or omission which may have directly or indirectly resulted in the events observed and reported by Comrade Captain Fritsch while engaged in the realisation of political-operational duties in the West German town of Meckenheim in the conurbation of Bonn. Furthermore, no acts of political-hostile diversion directed against-"

"Fine, Second Lieutenant," the major broke in. "You've made your point. But what do you *mean*?"

"What do I mean, Comrade Major Kühn?" I repeated, not understanding what he meant.

"What are your real conclusions? And don't repeat any of this manure." He waved the report at me again.

"From my analysis of the political-operational situation, I concluded that members of the Ministry who had operational contact with Source Bruno-"

"Yes, you said all that. But I want to know who's to *blame!*"

"Comrade Major ..." I paused, calculating risks and weighing words. "Comrade Major, I've seen only the written reports of some of the operatives. In order to complete my political-operational analysis, I request operational access to those operatives who had operational contact while Subject Bruno was in custody here in the Capital or in Building 74."

The major sucked his teeth and poked my report around the top of his desk. This was where I'd find out what his objectives were. Did he just want a scapegoat so he could draw a line under the affair? Or was he actually interested in finding out how the Bruno case had gone down the drain?

9
BERLIN FRIEDRICHSHAIN

"How long have I got before they come to get me?" Holger asked the following day.

"Don't be so melodramatic." It was nowhere near that bad. Not yet. "It's fine, really. I've got it all in hand."

That stiffened Holger's back a little and, satisfied with the effect my words had, I got up to make coffee.

It was Tuesday morning and I'd booked us into a safe flat in an old tenement overlooking the busy Warschauer Strasse. It was one of those places where the Firm politely requests the tenants make themselves scarce for a few hours, and they comply with a warm feeling in their hearts. Doing their bit for Socialism and the security of the Republic.

"You're sure you're not under observation?" I asked when I returned with the coffees. I wasn't being paranoid, it wasn't unknown for the Ministry to keep an eye on personnel—and to be blunt about it, Holger was under suspicion of, at best, cocking up a simple mission and at worst, having contact with the class enemy.

He shook his head, he hadn't noticed anyone following him.

"OK. Listen Holger, Major Kühn from ZAIG is in charge of the investigation. I asked for the files of everyone who had contact with Bruno, and for permission to interview them. So far I've only had the go-ahead to talk to the baby-sitters—I'll do that in the coming week. That includes you, of course."

"What about the officers who interrogated Bruno? They're the ones you need to look at!"

"One step at a time. You know how it works, Kühn isn't going to let me look at those files, not without good reason. I'm only a second lieutenant, the interrogators seriously outrank me."

Holger nodded. He wasn't dealing well with being under suspicion—it's not easy to continue as normal when you know the machinery of the Firm might move against you at any time, without warning. I'd experienced life in the Ministry's Hohenschönhausen remand prison myself, having been kept awake for days during never-ending interviews, enduring the inadequate portions of miserable food, the petty harassment by the guards, the more subtle persecutions by the interrogators—I wouldn't be too happy if someone told me I might be sent back there.

This is how we break people. This is what we do.

"Holger, stop worrying so much, pull yourself together. I'll work something out. In the meantime, I need you on your toes when I interview you tomorrow, last thing we need is someone reporting that you appeared nervous."

Holger nodded again.

"Keep your ear to the ground," I continued instructing him. "I need to hear about all the gossip in your department, any rumours, anything at all. We'll fix this, we'll dig you out of this hole." I leaned forward and patted Holger on the shoulder.

"Thanks, Reim," he replied. He even managed a smile. "It's good to know they're not about to come and get me."

"Don't worry, I'd tell you if it ever got that far."

But I wouldn't. If I did that I'd be risking my own freedom.

30

10
BERLIN LICHTENBERG

I started interviewing the babysitters the next morning. It was a friendly interrogation, no need for psychological pressure, so I invited *Gefreiter* Falk Nagel to my office rather than having him brought to a more formal interrogation room.

The corporal was small, just over the minimum height requirement, and when he sat down the buttons on his breast pockets just peeked over the top of my desk. I allowed him to make his report in his own words.

"Departure from Building 74 was scheduled for 0650 on the sixth of December. Situation at the time: patrol on the fence had no incidents to report, two hours before sunrise. Snow was on the ground as we left the compound," Nagel said.

I didn't know Building 74, I knew its codename and the fact that it was deep in the woods, somewhere between Beeskow and Briesen. I pictured the scene as Nagel spoke:

The endlessness of the pine forest was broken only by a simple chain link fence topped with barbed wire, behind which scuff-marks in the shallow snow showed the guards' patrol route. Out of sight of the fence, beyond yet more pines, a high wall hid an old forestry house and various outbuildings which had been added to accommodate larger groups, but the source and his briefing team hadn't needed much space.

There was only one gate in the wall, next to it a white globe lamp shone, replacing the full moon that had sunk beyond the trees an hour or two before. The lamp laid a bar over the glinting snow, a blue line from the front door to the shadows of the nearest trees.

"You'll be on the train soon, on your way home." The officer in charge had his right hand outstretched and his neck buried in the fleece collar of a padded parka.

"Are you sure this is the best way to do it?" Bruno took the hand and shook it, all the while looking around him, sniffing the frozen air.

"Just go back for a bit, test the water. See if you like the temperature. We'll never be too far away, any problems and we'll be there. If you think it's getting too hot, we'll bring you straight back," said the officer.

Bruno didn't answer. He followed a cleared pathway down some steps to a jetty and boarded a skiff held steady by Corporal Nagel.

Nagel punted the wooden boat across the river and climbed out, ready to open the door of a Wartburg. Bruno didn't look back at the house on the other side of the canal as the corporal got behind the steering wheel and put the car into gear. Bruno didn't look back as the car crumped over the snow and through a clearing. Bruno's gaze was focussed on the greyness cast by the headlights, the way they thrust aside the darkness that hung over the narrow track. The beam of the lights quivered and swerved as the car under-steered through the curves, rising onto the banks to either side, kicking up snow and sand as it went.

When they finally reached a metalled road, Bruno was still staring ahead. Corporal Nagel glanced in the rear-view mirror, wondering whether his charge wasn't quite awake yet, or perhaps nervous of returning to the West. It didn't make any difference to the corporal, his orders were to bring the asset to Beeskow railway station and make sure the next minders latched onto him.

They parked down the road from the station, engine running to keep the heater going. Articulated Ikarus buses lurched past, heavy diesel smoke mixing with the sharper tang of the Wartburg's exhaust.

"Time to go," said the corporal to the mirror, and watched Bruno fold up his tall frame to fit through the door.

He turned to take his suitcase, then stepped away from the car and picked his way down the ice-slick cobbles towards the station. With a sigh, the corporal got out and shut the back door, watching Bruno the whole time, only turning away once the shambling figure of the Westerner had reached the platform at which a three carriage train was standing.

When Corporal Nagel finished, I let him sit in silence for a moment or two. I had his written report in front of me, and I mentally ticked off each point, checking for agreement and discrepancy, omission or addition. This time the differences were all in omission: in his verbal report the corporal had given me nothing new but had left a few points out.

"The officer in charge, you say he was there to see Subject Bruno off?" I enquired.

"Yes, Comrade Second Lieutenant."

"His rank and name?"

"Oberleutnant Tinius of Main Department II."

I made a note then asked a few more questions I already knew the answer to. A few more notes, a bored expression on my face, then I began to circle in on a discrepancy I thought I had spotted:

"You parked the vehicle outside the bus garage of the VEB Verkehrskombinat Frankfurt?"

"Yes, Comrade Second Lieutenant."

"And you remained by your vehicle, watching the subject as he made his way to Beeskow station?"

"Yes, Comrade Second Lieutenant."

"You watched the subject the whole way, from the car to the train?"

"Yes, Comrade Second Lieutenant."

"You saw Subject Bruno board the train?"

"Comrade Second Lieutenant, I saw him on the platform ..."

I let him have some silence to think about what he'd just said. When it was obvious that the corporal wasn't going to complete his sentence, I pulled a town map of Beeskow from my desk drawer, folded it so the station was visible and asked him to show me where he'd parked.

He put his finger on the road outside the bus garage, just to the north of the station.

I flipped open another file and eased out a blueprint. It was a track layout diagram of the station. I slid it across the table towards the corporal then patiently waited for him to get his head round it.

"Was the train already standing at the platform when Subject Bruno arrived?" I asked.

"Yes, Comrade Second Lieutenant, scheduled arrival time was 0736, departure at 0753 and the subject reached the platform at 0749."

"At which platform was the train standing?"

The corporal examined the track diagram again. His face went pale as he realised why I was so interested in tracks and trains, his finger hesitated, but slowly it was drawn towards the platform on the south side of the station.

"When did you last see Subject Bruno?"

Again the finger dragged along the blueprint, this time ending up by the steps at the northern end of the pedestrian tunnel that led under the tracks.

"So, you saw the subject walk along the road and down into the underpass. You didn't see him come up the other side because the platform was hidden from view by the train. You didn't see him board the train, did you? And you didn't you see the comrades pick up his tail?"

I didn't wait for the corporal's answer, I stood up, took back the map and diagram and dismissed him.

Corporal Nagel had been negligent in following orders, but his negligence hadn't led to Bruno's arrest, this wouldn't be nearly enough to satisfy Kühn.

11
BERLIN LICHTENBERG

I sat at my desk, leafing through Private Rene Willich's report. It was a second, or even third, carbon copy and the letters were fuzzy, smeared across the rough paper, making them difficult to decipher.

According to what I was reading, Willich had been with Sergeant Georg Seyler that day, and I opened his report to compare both accounts.

Once I'd reminded myself of the pair's take on the mission, I took a greaseproof paper-wrapped sandwich and a flask of coffee out of my briefcase and enjoyed a second breakfast.

The operatives were in the corridor outside, ready for their interviews, but I didn't have a problem with making them wait a little.

Private Willich was young, his face was spotted with acne, yet his fair hair was already thinning on top. He stood at attention, fingers to his temple even though he wasn't wearing a cap.

"Genosse Unterleutnant, Soldat Willich auf Ihren Befehl zur Stelle!"

I never could stand crawlers, so I ignored him, continuing to examine the sparse report I'd already read twice. Then, without allowing him to sit down, I asked Willich to give me his verbal account.

Two operatives were in the second carriage, Willich sitting on the platform side, *Unteroffizier* Seyler across the aisle:

Bruno climbed the steps from the low platform and, looking

around, chose a free seat at the end. He heaved his luggage into the rack above the seat, the string webbing bellying down as the suitcase settled, then, without loosening his coat or scarf, Bruno sat down, cupping his hands against the window to peer out into the gloom of early morning.

The platform manager was waving a green lantern with one hand, closing the barrier to the platform with the other. A late passenger, mid-twenties, brown shoes and trousers, dark-grey overcoat, brown hair, no hat, ran up to the barrier, breathing heavily and arguing with the Reichsbahn employee, who kept his hand on the gate, holding it shut while watching the train pull out of the station.

Sergeant Seyler alighted at Kablow and was replaced by another operative. Willich left the train at the next stop.

Willich finished his statement, and I let him stand there for a bit longer. After a while I got bored and asked him a question.

"The passenger at Beeskow, the one who was late: your report doesn't identify him," I observed.

"No, Comrade Second Lieutenant."

"Why not?" I looked up for the first time since Willich had entered the room. He was standing at attention and staring at the wall above my head.

There was no answer, and I scribbled myself a note. I could make something of the omission, but to be fair it hadn't been Willich's responsibility to identify the passenger. The Operations Staff at the county administration should have made sure he had been tracked down and questioned. Maybe they did, but if so, the report hadn't been passed to me.

Unteroffizier Seyler was next. A more experienced operative who stood at attention until I let him sit down. His verbal report matched, word for word, what I had in the file in front of me. No, he hadn't seen the late passenger, he was engaged in operational-observation on the other side of the train,

36

keeping an eye on the traffic queueing up at the level crossing and watching passengers on the Fürstenwalde platform on the north side of the station.

I dismissed him and called for yet another grunt operative. This was the one who had accompanied Bruno between Zernsdorf and Königs Wusterhausen, replacing Seyler and Willich. I couldn't find any gaps in his account, no hint of any oversight or transgression. He'd sat in the same carriage as Bruno, alighted with him at Königs Wusterhausen station, followed him through the underpass and into the Mitropa buffet where he'd handed over to an operative already in place.

I sent him away and looked at my watch, deciding to deal with the final operative, the one from the Mitropa, before I went to the canteen. This afternoon I would interview Holger.

"Anything useful?" Holger asked as he sat down on the other side of my desk.

"Few minor discrepancies and oversights, nothing big enough to get you off the hook."

I held a deck of cigarettes over the table and Holger took one. He lit himself up and sucked hard, eyes down.

"You've got to pull yourself together," I told him. "Act like you're guilty and people will think you're guilty. Come on, shoulders back, head up."

Holger nodded, but remained slouched in the seat. I opened up the file, and tidied the papers in front of me, waiting for Holger.

"I've been told not to say about anything that happened at Building 74," he said to his lap. "I can only tell you about the train journey with Bruno that day."

"That's what we're here to talk about."

Holger stared at the top of my desk for a little longer then, without raising his head, began to talk:

Holger boarded the international express at Cottbus and

swept the train with another operative. A couple of Western pensioners were on board, otherwise only GDR citizens. They'd checked that the compartment reserved for Bruno was empty and retired to the last carriage in the train.

Arrival in Königs Wusterhausen was five minutes behind schedule, and Holger watched the passengers board.

"Every stop, scheduled or not, I stood by the window, kept an eye on who was getting on, who was getting off. No-one looked suspicious, no-one was out of place," he told me. "I went down the train once we'd left Magdeburg, checked Bruno was still in his seat. He was dozing, a book on his lap-"

"What was the book?" I interrupted. This was new information, not in the written report I had in front of me.

"Russian fairy tales."

"You could see that?"

"Next time I went past, the book was closed on the seat beside him, I could read the spine."

I noted the title and asked Holger to continue. Time enough to puzzle over this detail later.

"The train was virtually empty, only *Westlers* on the way home and a few of our pensioners visiting relatives."

"Tell me about the Westerners."

"Nobody stuck out. It was all old folk, I didn't pay much attention to them." Holger was sitting a little straighter now, caught up in his account, but he was still looking down at the hands clasped in his lap.

"As far as I could tell, they all left the train before Cologne. Once we crossed the border, the train filled up and it was hard to keep track of individual passengers."

"Any incidents at the border?"

"Not as far as I could tell. I couldn't exactly stick my head out of the window while customs and the Pass and Control Unit were checking the train. But I can tell you Bruno definitely wasn't pulled off."

"Any contact with other passengers while you were going

through West Germany?"

Bruno lifted his shoulders and let them drop. "I went through the train again after Braunschweig. The reservation slips on Bruno's compartment had been removed, presumably by the West German conductor. A young lady was sitting opposite Bruno. They weren't talking. In fact, Bruno seemed to be dozing again."

"What about other operatives on the train?"

"As far as I know, I was the only one on board after Magdeburg. Or do you know differently?"

I didn't. That is to say, I hadn't been given any reports by watchers operating on the train once it had crossed into West Germany. I made a note to double check, and another to remind myself to find out who else had held exit visas valid for travel on that train.

"How's the wife?" I asked.

Not expecting the change of subject, Holger glanced up, then quickly down again.

"And the kid—Hannes, isn't it? How's Hannes?

"Got his *Jugendweihe* coming up next spring, doing the classes, already got a suit for the ceremony. He can't wait for all the presents."

I nodded, not really interested in his son's coming-of-age ceremony, I just wanted Holger to relax a bit. The last thing I needed was for him to slouch out of my office, looking like a guilty man, not if I was going to tell Major Kühn that Captain Holger Fritsch was innocent.

While my friend talked about his son and how proud Ilona, the wife and mother, was, I turned my attention to the bottom drawer and pulled out a couple of glasses and a bottle.

"Chin up," I told Holger. "We'll get it sorted. Just act normal, OK?" I handed over a glass, brimful with clear alcohol.

We held our glasses up and, for the first time that day, he looked me in the eye.

"To keeping you off the hook!" I toasted.

12
BERLIN LICHTENBERG

I went to see Holger after work the next day. He lived in a block opposite a self-service market on Gounodstrasse. I rang the bell and he came down to let me in, surprise written all over his face.

"Are you meant to be here?" he asked, peering up and down the street, checking whether the neighbours had spotted me.

"Let's go upstairs," I suggested as I squeezed past him and started up the steps. "Which floor?"

Holger and his family were on the top floor of a four storey concrete block, same design as I lived in except he had a three-room flat.

He ushered me down the narrow hallway and I caught a glimpse of his wife moving around in the kitchen as I went past.

In the living room, a standard lamp in the corner cast yellow light over a brown couch and armchairs. Brassy lametta decorated the moulding at the top of the walls. A listless spruce loitered in one corner, waiting to be hung with baubles and festive lights.

"Relax," I told Holger as I shut the door. "Kühn gave me permission to take a closer look at all of you. If anyone is curious enough to ask, I'll tell them that's why I'm here."

Holger sank onto the couch, clasping his hands in his lap. He remained like that, examining his hands, so I opened the door to the hall.

"A beer?" I asked, but didn't wait for an answer, just headed around the corner to the kitchen.

A surprise was waiting for me. Holger's wife was standing in the doorway, wiping her hands on a flowery pinny. But it wasn't her presence that had unsettled me, it was her looks.

"You must be a colleague of Holger's?" she enquired, holding her now-dry hand out for me to shake.

"Reim," I managed to answer, holding my own hand out.

Her long fingers clasped mine. Her skin was soft and her smile was adorable. And her eyes—her eyes were such a deep blue it felt like I was staring into the Baltic sky on a clear summer's evening. I'm sorry if I'm telling this like I read it in a cheap romance magazine, but that's how it felt at the time.

"Why don't you give me my hand back? That way I can get you a coffee—or would you prefer a beer?" That smile again.

I let go of her hand and watched as she fetched a couple of bottles from the fridge, took the bottle opener from a hook and put everything on a tray with a couple of glasses.

"Are you stopping for tea? It's just potato salad and sausage, but you're very welcome to join us." She gave me the tray.

"No, I can't stop long." I retreated down the hall, wondering where Holger had been hiding his wife all this time.

In the living room, Holger was still staring at his hands and didn't notice me take a deep breath.

"Here's your beer." I clinked bottles with him and we drank from the neck, leaving the glasses where they were on the tray.

"You've been ordered to take a closer look at me?" Holger asked after a sip or two.

"No. I asked for it—like I said, it makes it easier for us to meet without raising suspicion."

Holger didn't show any signs of hearing what I'd just said, he took another sip of beer then stared out of the window. You could see the flat roof of the supermarket from here, ventilators set into a wrinkled, tar-paper surface.

"I came to tell you that I've handed in my preliminary report, there's no good reason to suspect any of the babysitting team. I did find a few holes in the others' accounts, just to show willing. But you're in the clear."

"Why wouldn't I be in the clear?" Holger came to life, his eyes swivelled around to meet mine. They were deep in his head, dark tunnels that spoke of sleepless nights. "It was the mole that shopped Bruno, I told you that. Someone on the interrogation team! So what are you doing about it? That's where you should be looking."

"The squirrel feeds slowly-" I began, but Holger cut me off.

"Don't start quoting idioms at me! I know you're taking things slowly, but can't you see I'm worried? Not just for me, but for Ilona and Hannes, I've got them to think about, too."

I held my hands up, appealing for calm. When Holger's gaze dropped again, I told him how the meeting with Major Kühn had gone, that he'd given me a bit of leeway to do some more digging.

"He won't let me talk to the interrogation team. You can understand that, can't you? It's a rank thing—he won't even let me read their cadre files, never mind the interrogation transcripts."

"So you're not going to be much use in finding this mole, are you?"

I looked away. Holger had hit the nail on the head. Bit ungracious, perhaps, but he wasn't wrong.

13
BERLIN LICHTENBERG

The coffee was weak and sour, the slice of ham was as gristly as the dry bread roll it was hiding in. I prodded my breakfast again and decided to leave it on the table.

Back in my office, I considered what Holger had said to me the night before. I still thought he was right: even if there was a mole in the Ministry I wasn't going to get anywhere near him unless I stopped wasting my time interviewing the babysitters and started doing some proper investigating. A West German mole wouldn't be somebody in the lower ranks, tasked with basic operational activities. He'd be higher up, somebody with access to files, somebody involved in operational planning.

I should write that in the new report I was preparing for Major Kühn, it would make for more interesting reading than the trivial infractions I'd uncovered so far. There are only so many ways you can say: *things weren't done exactly by the book, but there's no reason to suspect the babysitters have done anything which might have compromised Bruno's legend.*

Right now my biggest headache was that I had to find something new to report on. I'd asked for more leeway in investigating the babysitters as a way to provide cover for my regular chats with Holger, but now it was time for me to justify that request. I couldn't deliver a report less than twenty-four hours later saying there was no point in doing any more digging, thank you very much. Like it or not, I'd have to put a bit more effort into this, if only to fill a few more pages in the file.

With a sigh, I got up from my desk and headed for the registry.

I arrived at the archives by way of Kühn's secretary, where I picked up the paperwork I needed. I shoved the stamped and signed chit across the archivist's desk, it was a request for the files of all the people holding an exit visa issued for the train Bruno was on the day he headed back to Bonn.

The archivist sucked his teeth for a bit, then told me to come back the next day.

That was fine, I had another stamped and signed chit, this one demanded an express service. The archivist nodded and was back within ten minutes, holding a thin file and a place card.

"The files are out, ZAIG/II have them. Should have come back a few days ago," the archivist grumbled. He slid the file across the counter, keeping hold of the place card. It was upside down, and his hand obscured most of it, but I managed to read the name of the lender: Major Kühn.

I sat at one of the desks and opened the file. It was an appendix to one I already had in my office, the one withdrawn by Kühn before he passed it on to me. A lot of what was in this file was the same as in the copy I had spent so many hours reading and re-reading. Some new information had been added though, presumably it had been filed since Kühn withdrew the main file.

One of the new additions was a full list of babysitters on Bruno's case that day.

I checked the list, mentally ticking off those I had already interviewed. They were all there, all except for a couple of new names, names of operatives who had been on the express train to Cologne after it crossed the border into West Germany. I made a note of those names then took the file back and requested the cadre files for the two babysitters I'd just found out about.

This was interesting, at least on a theoretical level, but

really it was just more material to follow up and pad my report with. I was about to return the file when a circulation list attached to the document caught my eye: Holger's name was on there, and he'd initialled it to acknowledge sight of the document.

I stared at the circulation list. It was evidence: only a couple of days previously, Holger had sworn that he didn't know whether he was the only operative on that train after it left Marienborn.

14
BERLIN LICHTENBERG

I withdrew the cadre files of the two new babysitters and took them back to my office then went up to the brass's corridor.

"Where can I find a West German train timetable?" I asked Kühn's secretary.

"I haven't got one." She glared at me as if I'd made an indecent suggestion.

"I realise that, Comrade Ehrlich, but I thought perhaps you'd have an idea where I might find such a thing?" I said it as sweetly as I could. Any sweeter and I'd be choking on my own vomit.

"Try Administration Rear Services," she suggested after another scowl.

I tried Administration Rear Services, who sent me to the travel department. It took me half an hour and quite a few of my skills of persuasion to get hold of a copy of the West German Bundesbahn timetable. It was a heavy thing, much thicker than the Reichsbahn version, and I had to look at several pages before I found what I was looking for: International express D444, Görlitz to Cologne via Marienborn and Helmstedt.

I was interested in whether it had any long stops while in West Germany, long enough for Bruno to get off the train and make a phone call before getting back on and continuing his journey. But on inspection, I could see the only stop longer than four minutes was at the first station after the border. In Helmstedt, the Reichsbahn locomotive from the East is uncoupled and a Bundesbahn engine attached—that takes time, enough time to leave the train for a few minutes.

I copied the timetable information into my notebook and went back to my office to look at the cadre files of the pair of babysitters who'd accompanied Bruno and Holger on the journey to Cologne.

They both had standard backgrounds. Both pretty much at the start of their careers, just a few years experience. Both had wives and children who could remain in the country as security when the husbands went West on the job. One had done his national service on the border, the other in the barracked police reserves, the *VP-Bereitschaften.* Both were Party members, and until they'd reached 25 years of age had both remained in the FDJ youth organisation. There was nothing to commend or criticise the pair for—no black marks against them. But I still decided to call them in for a chat.

After a couple of hours of picking at their stories, I wasn't any further. They'd sat in different compartments in the same carriage as Bruno, had regularly checked on his status as they walked up and down the aisle, ostensibly on the way to the toilet or the buffet car. Bruno had spent his time looking out of the window, reading what looked like a children's book or dozing.

"Tell me about the book," I demanded.

"Yellow cover. Large writing and pen and ink illustrations, about this big," replied the second babysitter, holding his hands twenty centimetres apart. He was a rotund corporal with fair hair and a brush moustache.

"And the subject didn't have any other reading materials?"

"No, Comrade Second Lieutenant, apart from a newspaper."

That made me sit up. Nobody had mentioned a newspaper before. "When did he read a newspaper?"

The corporal looked like he was going to scratch his head, but had enough discipline to keep his hands down. It took him ten seconds or so to answer. "After Hannover, before Herford," he decided. "The sun was going down, I remember seeing the subject tilt the newspaper to the window to catch the light so he could see more clearly."

I flipped my notebook open and checked the times the train stopped in Hannover: 1553, and Herford: 1659. The sun went down just after four o'clock at this time of year. Corroboration, of a sort.

"Tell me about the newspaper. What was it, East or West? Was he reading it or doing the crossword? Where did he get it from?"

Another pause while the corporal thought about it. "I don't know, Comrade Second Lieutenant."

I dismissed him and told him to send the other babysitter in again, but that one hadn't seen Bruno reading a newspaper at all.

The newspaper could have come from anywhere. The explanation might be simple and innocent: another passenger had left it behind, or Bruno had bought it in the Mitropa cafe in Königs Wusterhausen.

And the not so innocent explanations? Bruno left the train at some point to buy the paper from a kiosk on the platform. The paper contained a message, it was passed on by another passenger—or even the conductor.

15
BERLIN LICHTENBERG

I wanted this report off my desk. The case wasn't going anywhere and I had nothing to say that I hadn't said before: there was no reason to suspect Bruno's babysitters of selling him out.

At least I had enough new material to justify the extension; I had interviewed the two babysitters who hadn't appeared in the original collated reports, and I had the new information about the newspaper that Bruno had been reading.

If Major Kühn was a bastard he'd throw the report back at me, tell me to track down the man who missed the train in Beeskow and order me to find out how Bruno got hold of the newspaper he'd been reading between Hannover and Herford.

I'd finished typing and was wondering whether to deliver my words of wisdom to the secretary before I went home, or whether it could wait until Monday. I slid it into a cardboard folder and was writing out the details on the front when Holger knocked and came in. I was bored and tired of the day, the last thing I needed was to let Holger drag my mood down even further.

But when I glanced up I had to take a second look. My friend was leaning over my desk, hands resting on the chipboard surface. His eyes glittered with energy.

"Drink?" I offered, wondering what had happened.

"Thought you'd never ask!" This was more like the Holger I knew.

I pulled the bottle and glasses from the bottom drawer and

poured out a couple of measures. As I handed his glass over, Holger looked me in the eye and proposed a toast:

"To success!"

I met his eye and asked him which particular kind of success we were drinking to.

"Success in finding out what happened to Bruno, of course."

I took a swallow of *Doppelkorn* and thought how to respond, but Holger started talking without any prompting.

"Have you finished the report for Major Kühn?" he asked.

"Wasn't much to add." I patted the folder in front of me. "But since you ask, when you were on the train to Cologne, did you notice Bruno reading a newspaper?"

Holger reached for the bottle and added a dash more to his glass, holding it up and raising his eyebrows in query.

"No, why?" he said once he'd had a taste of the schnapps.

"Just something one of the other babysitters said."

"Between Königs Wusterhausen and the border?" Holger frowned.

"No, on the other side. After Hannover."

"Listen, Reim: you've been good to me these last couple of weeks. I wanted to say thank you. Why don't you come round for tea? Ilona would like to meet you properly."

It was a gracious offer, and the thought of seeing Ilona again made me want to accept. But I declined. It wasn't my thing, going to a colleague's for supper, particularly not colleagues I was officially investigating. And anyway, I was wondering why the change of subject.

"No, you must come. I told Ilona you'd say no, and she commanded I insist." He stood up and clicked his heels, as if he'd just received an order from a superior officer.

"OK," I capitulated. "But only on condition you tell me why you're so chipper all of a sudden. Last night you weren't looking so optimistic."

"I realised I had nothing to worry about. I've got you on my side, and you've already told the major that there's no evidence against me. So why am I worrying?" He looked at his glass while he said this, the words and his tone of voice were convincing, but nothing else about him was. "Besides," he continued. "I reckon I've got a lead on this mole."

16
BERLIN WEISSENSEE

I arrived in Weissensee with a bottle of Russian Champagne for Ilona and a bottle of Schilkin vodka for Holger.

"*Sovietskoye Shampanskoye!*" Ilona cried when she saw the Crimean sparkling wine. She gave me a kiss on the cheek before taking the bottle into the kitchen. I heard the fridge door open.

"Reim, in here." Holger gestured from the living room.

I went in and put the vodka on the dining table next to the Christmas tree. Since I was last here the decorations had been hung and the lights switched on. I looked at the twinkling tree, bright and colourful, and thought back to the only time we'd had one in our flat. My wife, Renate, had brought it home the first winter after we married and I'd made such a fuss about outdated Christian superstitions and the duty of Party members to agitate against such pernicious bourgeois traditions that she'd never bothered again. And now she was gone.

Behind me, the clink of a bottle told me I was about to get some of the vodka I'd brought. I turned around in time to take a glass from Holger and we looked each other in the eye as we threw back the alcohol, Russian style.

"With good vodka you need food—a slice of black bread ..." Holger said in a mock Russian accent.

"Don't overdo it—just hold it next to the glass," I replied, hamming it up just as Holger had.

Holger burst into laughter, and I grinned, remembering the KGB colonel we were mimicking—he'd once given us a lecture on co-operation between the fraternal socialist forces for peace.

"Do they really say that, about the black bread, do you think?" Holger wondered as he left the room.

A moment later he was back with a couple of cold Wernesgrüner beers. "Hannes is at some FDJ thing so it'll just be the three of us tonight. Sit down, make yourself comfy."

Instead of sitting down, I went into the hall and turned left to get to the kitchen, pausing to admire the view as Ilona bent down to fetch some plates out of a cupboard.

"Anything I can do to help?"

"Could you take the tray in?" She gave me a smile that warmed my insides in a way vodka alone could never do. "You're a darling—Holger would never think to ask."

Normally, I'd never have thought to ask either, but for one of Ilona's smiles ... I carried the tray through, shaking my head at my giddiness.

I laid the table while Holger watched me with a smile on his own face, but it didn't have half the effect his wife's had.

"It's very simple, I'm afraid," Ilona said as she brought a steaming tureen into the living room and set it down in the middle of the table. "Just potato soup with sausage. Holger didn't give me any notice at all, and by the time I got to the *Kaufhalle*, they'd sold out of anything interesting."

Holger lit a cigarette as Ilona cleared the table.

"I wish you wouldn't do that—why don't you go out on the balcony?" she muttered.

Holger ignored her and offered me the deck and a box of matches. I lit up as Holger went to the living room door.

"We're going to need a bit of peace and quiet here," he called as he shut the door.

I sucked on my cigarette while I waited for Holger to make the first move. Whatever was coming, it was the reason I'd been invited for dinner.

"You found another couple of babysitters?" he asked.

I nodded and took the bottle of beer he'd opened for me. There was silence for a moment or two, then I told him how I'd found out about them.

"Funny thing is, your name was on the distribution list, so you should have known about them."

"Must have missed that one." Holger took a puff of his cigarette and followed it up with a swig from the bottle. "How long were they with us for?"

"Cologne. After that it was just you and Bruno."

Holger looked thoughtful for a moment or two, then put his next question. "So you've interviewed all of us babysitters, right? What did the others say?"

If I'd been debriefing Holger a couple of days previously, he was now effectively interviewing me, wanting to hear everything I'd found out over the last week. I was uncomfortable about it, but I told myself that the reason I'd been so conscientious in this investigation was to clear my friend's name, so it made sense to fill him in on what I'd learnt.

After the beer was finished and the vodka had made a reappearance, I asked Holger about his current theories about the mole. Whatever he'd found out had been good enough to cheer him up, so it was worth hearing.

But Holger wasn't having any of it. "You'll have to leave this with me for a bit—you know how it is, source protection and all that."

"Just tell me in general terms."

"Not possible. I'll tell you about it as soon as I can." If he was trying for reassuring, he hadn't succeeded.

17
BERLIN LICHTENBERG

I'd handed in my report last thing on Friday, just before leaving the Centre, and since then hadn't heard from Major Kühn. But my new department had finally taken note of my existence and I was ordered to report to Captain Dupski. The captain, a slight man with regulation cropped hair and a non-regulation stammer, provided me with a stack of files to tidy up so they could be archived.

The work wasn't challenging, but it kept me out of trouble.

By Wednesday, I'd begun wondering why there'd been no word from Holger. Hadn't he promised to tell me about this new lead he had on the mole? For the rest of the afternoon, in between comparing files and marking duplicate reports for destruction, I played around with the idea of going to see Holger, finding out what he knew. It irked me, all I'd done for him and now he was keeping information from me.

On the other hand, some instinct from deep inside—the self-preservatory one that I usually ignore—told me I'd done my part. I'd helped Holger as much as I could and there was no need to encourage him further.

It was mid-afternoon when my phone rang; I was to report to Captain Dupski.

"*Kegeln*," he announced before I was even properly through the door. "You're a bowler—says so here in your cadre file."

"With respect, Comrade Captain, I'm a poor bowler." It's true, during my last posting with HA VI, I had been in the *Kegelteam*, but only because some sort of social engagement with other members of the unit had been expected. They'd tossed balls around and knocked down wooden kegels or dolls or whatever they're called and I got the drinks in.

"Well, as long as you know ..." he paused to allow his stammer to settle. "As long as you know how to hold a ball— we're a man short and we have a match against HA II/2 tomorrow evening. We need to win."

Audience effectively over, I left the captain's office with instructions to see the *Feldwebel* down the corridor.

"Practice tonight at 1900," he told me. "You know where the bowling alley is? Next to the barbers in House 18."

Good job I didn't have any plans for the evening.

Bowling was no fun, and that was no surprise. Maybe I could have used it as an opportunity to get to know others in my unit, but they were all best of pals, the banter had already started, there were wives and girlfriends to ask after and joke about. I was the new boy, only there to make up the numbers because Lieutenant Hötschelt had injured himself.

Things might have been different if I'd been any good at bowling, but my poor performance excluded me from the bawdy jokes about how Hötschelt had sprained his wrist.

So I rolled the ball towards the skittles, glad if I managed to make contact at all, and brooded over how scarce Holger had managed to make himself since the weekend.

The bowling alley was booked for the whole of the evening, but after they'd seen me in action, the team left me on the bench.

"Match tomorrow at 1900, doesn't matter if you forget to come," said First Lieutenant Willems, the team captain, after an hour. A dismissal if ever I've heard one.

I didn't bother answering, I put my head down and left, walking down Ruschestrasse, turning right at the bottom and heading for the tram stop on Jacques-Duclos-Strasse. Without thinking about it, I ended up on the tram to Weissensee. Since

I was already on my way, I decided to carry on and see whether Holger was at home.

"Comrade Reim!" Ilona greeted me with a kiss on the cheek. She seemed pleased to see me, and that was enough to make me pleased to see her. "Come on up, don't let the weather in."

I followed her up the stairs, I was pretty sure she was moving her behind more than she strictly needed to.

"Holger at home?" I asked as she let me into the flat.

"It's Wednesday, Kegel practice night."

"He's on the team?"

"Big match tomorrow."

Ilona was waiting to take my coat, and without thinking I slipped it off and gave it to her.

"Coffee?" she asked. "Or something stronger?" Was that a wink she just gave me?

Without waiting for an answer, she disappeared into the kitchen, returning a moment later with chilled sparkling wine, the Russian stuff I'd brought last Friday. "Let's open this, Holger doesn't appreciate *Shampanskoye.*"

Ilona came towards me, backing me into the living room. We went past a closed door, a poster of an album cover: the Puhdys' *Computer-Karriere.*

"Hannes?" I asked, nodding at the door.

"Sleepover at a friend's."

"On a school night?" I asked, immediately feeling a little pompous.

Ilona had manoeuvred me to the couch by now, and with a gentle shove on my chest, she pushed me down.

"So, Comrade Reim," she murmured. Then, in her normal voice, the one she used on Holger. "I can't go on calling you Comrade Reim, that's ridiculous. What do your friends call you?"

"Reim," I said, looking at her bosom, just a few centimetres from my face. "Everyone calls me Reim." She had her head tipped to one side, her soft hair fell over one eye.

With a smile, she held the bottle out for me. "Would you? I do think opening champagne is best done by a man."

I popped the cork, and it bounced off somewhere behind the Christmas tree. Ilona had the glasses at the ready, and I drizzled the wine into them.

"When's Holger due back?" I asked.

"Oh, he won't be back before midnight. Sometimes he doesn't come home at all after practice."

I put the bottle down, and Ilona gave me a glass. She held hers up for me to clink, and she made her big eyes even larger, looking deep inside me.

"So, as you can see, we're all by ourselves."

18
BERLIN FRIEDRICHSHAIN

I skipped breakfast the next morning—my stomach felt like it had been force-fed sauerkraut; when I belched, the foul vapours even tasted of rotten cabbage. Add in the panzers rolling around inside my skull, and you'll understand why I didn't fancy my chances against a hard-boiled egg.

I managed a large glass of water, and in my book that counted as progress. It was enough to encourage me to head to the office.

I took the U-Bahn, a mistake that almost lost me the glass of water. The shrieking of wheels on rails was bad enough, but what almost did for me was the stink of the workers pressed into the wagon: body odour, stale sweat, musty clothes—all mixed in with the pervasive tang of brown coal ash.

Most passengers left the train at Frankfurter Allee, and I got off with a few other Ministry employees at the next stop. The climb up the steps to the road was the signal for the panzers to go on manoeuvres again, and when I reached the cold air of the street, I stood still for a moment, feeling sweat ooze from beneath the brim of my hat.

I've never believed in divine retribution, I leave that stuff to the bourgeoisie in the West. Crimean champagne and I had never got on, simple as that. But Ilona had been insistent. And that smile.

I groaned at the memory. Last night. Just too much *Shampanskoye*, I told myself. And the beer after that must have come from a bad batch.

I had no shame about what happened after the sparkling

wine and the bad beer. Ilona had been in the driving seat and I had been a willing passenger. No, it wasn't a guilty conscience about sleeping with Holger's wife that was tormenting me—there was something else, pulling at the edge of my mind.

Must be the hangover.

Having safely reached my office, I broke the seal on my safe and took several folders out, opening them at random and spreading them across my desk.

I stepped back and considered the arrangement. It looked convincing enough. Sitting down, I leaned back and closed my eyes, hoping sleep would release me from my griping stomach and my rolling head.

But I couldn't sleep. It was there again, that vague tugging at the sheet of memory, causing wrinkles to appear, all pointing to what had happened with Ilona. Had I grown a conscience overnight?

That was a disturbing thought. If it were true then I could give up the business of being an officer of the Stasi right now.

Let's not overreact, Reim, I told myself. *It's just the bloody Shampanskoye.*

I was awake the instant the door clicked open—it takes years of practice to be this good. By the time Captain Dupski appeared, I was standing and doing a good impression of looking alert.

Without a word, Dupski strode across the room and opened the window. Traffic noise and fumes seeped through the gap along with the cold air.

"As you were, Comrade Second Lieutenant," he said.

"Comrade Captain!" I replied. But I couldn't sit down because he was still standing there.

"You ready for tonight?"

I might be capable of jumping to attention from a state of deep slumber, but my brain was still catching up.

"Bowling." The captain did something with his thin eyebrows, something very effective at showing disapproval. "You were at training last night? Ready for the match? We need a good showing against ... against the HA II team," he stammered, as if winning the bowling match meant a great deal to him.

I dropped my pencil and must have looked gormless because the captain moved his eyebrows around a bit more. Bowling? Was that what had been bothering me? I pushed the thought aside and concentrated on my superior. "*Jawohl*, Comrade Captain!"

"Relying on you, Comrade Second Lieutenant," he said as he left the room, leaving the door ajar.

I didn't get up to shut it, I sank into my seat. Bowling practice. Holger was at bowling practice last night.

"Where did he go to for practice?" I asked myself, half-aloud. Where had his team trained? Because my department had booked the alley for the whole evening.

19
BERLIN LICHTENBERG

We were all in civvies, having changed out of uniform before coming to the bowling alley. All that remained to do was to put our bowling shoes on and give each other encouraging slaps on the back. With jaunty words we began to march into the bowling alley. I hung back, and the team captain, First Lieutenant Willems, a fellow who obviously invested a large part of his pay packet in growing an already impressive beer belly, stood in the doorway, gesturing impatiently at me.

I followed the comrades in and watched the team from HA II/2 enter from the opposite door—Holger and Corporal Nagel, one of Bruno's babysitters, among them. I pulled Willems back into the changing room.

"One of their team members—I have a professional interest ..." I whispered.

Willems peered through the door at the other team. There was no need to explain what I meant, we were both from ZAIG/II, investigating disciplinary lapses was our work.

"We could tell them to retire the player?" he suggested.

"I'm not allowed to tell you which one it is." I shook my head. "Besides, if I don't take part then you could ask them to stand down one of their team members to keep the numbers even."

Willems scratched his head and peered around the edge of the door frame, sizing up the competition. I was such a poor player that losing me from the team was no great loss, and if he could persuade the other team to play with just five men then we had better chances of going through to the next round. It wasn't a hard decision.

"Go on then, but if we lose tonight then you'll have some explaining to do in the morning—Comrade Captain Dupski is keen for a good result."

He nodded towards the doorway, and I moved to one side to look into the bowling alley. In the shadows at the back, in full uniform, sat the lean figure of Dupski.

Half an hour later I was in a colourless bar near Boxhagener Platz in Friedrichshain. I had a table to myself and a beer in front of me—I'm a simple man, easily pleased.

I wasn't interested in a bowling match, felt far more comfortable here in this anonymous bar. But was there more to it than that? I'd only reached my decision to skip the match when I saw Holger. I knew he'd be there, Ilona had told me he was on the Kegel team, and I knew it was his division we were playing, so it wasn't hard to do the maths. But when he walked into the bowling alley, I'd also known I couldn't face him.

I had to ask myself whether I *was* feeling guilty about cuckolding him the previous night but I chuckled about the idea of guilt, then my thoughts took me to Captain Dupski.

Whether or not the ZAIG/II team lost the match, I'd have my superior officer on my case tomorrow morning. He had ordered me to make up the numbers on the team and I hadn't turned up. But if he kicked off, I could just tell him to ask Major Kühn for the reason why I couldn't play against one or more members of the HA II/2 team. Cast iron alibi.

Unless Dupski was a very foolish man, the matter would end there. At least until the next match.

I lifted my glass and wished Lieutenant Hötschelt's wrist a speedy recovery.

20
BERLIN LICHTENBERG

Dupski collared me in the corridor the next afternoon.

"Finished with those files yet, Comrade Reim?"

I informed him of my progress in laborious detail and smothering a smirk when his eyes began to lose focus.

"Yes, well. There are more files that need sorting in the secretariat, pick them up when you're done with this lot," he said over his shoulder as he headed towards the stairwell.

Mission accomplished. And he hadn't even raised the matter of the bowling match.

Back in my office, I opened one of the files on my desk then went to stand by the window. I didn't have much of a view— an inner courtyard with little foot-traffic. Somewhere in the building opposite was the big boss's office. If Comrade General Mielke got bored of his work and went to stand by his window, he would see me staring back at him. The thought was enough to send me back to my desk.

I'd finished with the files, but wasn't about to go and exchange them for some more. No, I'd sit here, drinking coffee from the Thermos flask and combing the *Neues Deutschland* for clues about what was actually going on in our half of the world. The front page told me it was Friday. Not just any Friday, but the day before Christmas Eve.

The calendar had been kind to us this year—Christmas Eve on a Saturday, first Christmas Day on Sunday. This time there would be no overt conflict between family and Firm, no choice to be made about whether to spend Christmas Eve feasting on roast goose and unwrapping presents with the children or pretending it was a normal day at Berlin Centre.

Of course, it meant we'd all have to be back at our desks on the second Christmas Day, Monday the 26th of December, but I'm sure even the least enthusiastic colleagues would be glad to escape the family festivities by then.

I had no such conflict to resolve. My wife had left me over a year ago, and despite having come back for a week or two in the autumn, she was out of my life again. For good this time. There was no-one nagging me about being at home during the festival, I had no-one at home discouraging me from spending the whole weekend at the office, sending notes through the internal mail system to prove how diligently present and active I'd been while everyone else was drinking themselves senseless under the family Christmas tree.

I was still weighing up the idea of spending the festive period under my desk with a bottle of schnapps when Holger came for a visit.

"Should you be here?" I asked as he came through the door. I checked my watch, then got the bottle out of the drawer.

"Thought you'd finished with the case, passed it back to your Captain Kranich or whatever he's called."

"Kühn," I replied absently, reaching for a glass that had slid to the back of the drawer. "But whether or not I've finished with the case, you promised to tell me about this lead you were following up?"

Holger didn't answer immediately, he'd sat down and was showing a lot of interest in the way I was measuring alcohol into the two glasses. We did the usual holding of the glasses in mid-air while fixing the other with our eyes. It was a silent toast this time.

"Dead end." He finally responded to my question. "Didn't come to anything."

"But this whole Bruno thing, it is still bothering you?" I guessed. "Seriously, I don't think you have anything to worry about—there's nothing in any of my reports that could be used against you. Whatever the reason for Bruno's arrest, we won't find it by going over what happened that day."

"Doesn't it bother you? The idea that there may be a mole?" Bruno asked, toying with his glass. He was pretty much back to his old self. A bit slower, shoulders still hunched, but nothing like the depressed wreck he'd been the other week.

I topped up our glasses again, another silent toast.

"What evidence do we have that there's a mole? Bruno said so, that's it. Bruno who's doing something about the RAF—not even remotely involved in anything to do with the GDR."

"You're right, I shouldn't let it bother me, I should let things take their course." Holger took another sip. "But there is one thing I can't get my head round. Why did they arrest Bruno as soon he got home? If they had intelligence that he'd defected then it would have made more sense to watch and wait. Use him to channel misinformation in our direction, perhaps even turn him into a double agent. But arresting him immediately? That's just amateur."

"Perhaps they didn't know he'd defected? Maybe he's been arrested for something completely different—something he did before he even came to visit his relatives last month."

"Precisely!" Holger tapped his empty glass on my desk. "It's as good as proof that they don't suspect Bruno of defecting."

"Which means you can stop worrying about the idea of a mole," I murmured, looking at my watch and wondering whether it was home time yet.

"Ah, Heym—I wanted to talk to you," announced Major Kühn.

I reached the main door to the building just as he was coming in, flanked by lackeys in uniform and some kind of clerk in civvies.

"Not a fence-sitter are you? No room in my section for fence-sitters." He told me, his entourage bunching up in the doorway, pretending not to listen.

"No, Comrade Major. Not known as a fence-sitter."

"Well, your reports make you sound like a fence-sitter. Why haven't you come down on one side or the other?"

The major's criticism was undeserved, and I began to push back. "With respect, Comrade Major-"

"Never mind." He was about to sweep on, but something made me intervene. Injured pride, probably.

"Comrade Major, permission to speak?"

Kühn paused, his brow wrinkled. I glared at his escort until they dropped back a pace or two.

"Just something that came to mind, Comrade Major, I couldn't put it in an operational report. Merely conjecture, but I think it's worth mentioning."

The Major manoeuvred his bulky body round until he was facing me. His flunkeys took another step back, most of them were now standing in the sleet that was falling beyond the entry doors.

"Subject Bruno was arrested on his own doorstep. If the West Germans had operational awareness of the offer he made to us, well, they wouldn't have arrested him on sight. If the situation were the other way round ..." The major bristled at the very notion that one of ours could have defected. "We would have watched and waited until we found an advantage to exploit. To me, Source Bruno's arrest casts doubt on the idea that someone in this building is engaging in political-operational diversionary tactics."

"Are you suggesting there's a possibility that the West Germans were tipped off by someone on our side?" Kühn's brow lowered, making his eyes recede even further.

"Comrade Major, my intention was to disprove the theory-" I wasn't allowed to finish. With a wave at his lackeys, Kühn continued down the corridor.

"Come and see me tomorrow at 1100 hours, Comrade Second Lieutenant Heym," he said over his shoulder.

That was Christmas Eve sorted, then.

21
BERLIN LICHTENBERG

Christmas Eve at 1058 hours found me standing in the corridor, left wrist held up so I could see my watch, right hand poised to knock on Major Kühn's office door.

1059 hours. I waited for the second hand to sweep down to the bottom of the dial, then knocked.

"*Herein.*"

I entered, and without looking at the officers around the table, reported my presence to the major.

"Sit down, Comrade Second Lieutenant, you're early."

Resisting the urge to take a pointed look at my watch, I slid into an empty chair and did a cautious sweep of the assembled personages. Sitting next to Kühn was another major, his fair hair slick with oil. He kept his body angled slightly away from his neighbour, as if he wasn't comfortable in Kühn's presence.

Between the major and myself was a captain. Limp moustache, dandruff on his shoulders, generally running to seed. On my other side was a first lieutenant, and of the three unknown officers, he was the youngest and keenest. His head bobbed along to whatever was being said, his eyes fixed on whoever happened to be speaking.

"I think we should keep the file open—at least pending the gathering of further operational intelligence," the blond major was saying, taking care never to look directly at Kühn.

The first lieutenant to my right nodded enthusiastically and the captain's eyes were lowered, as if he were checking the size of the bulge his belly made beneath his uniform tunic.

"Let's not get ahead of ourselves, Comrade Major," Kühn

interrupted. "Comrade Second Lieutenant Heym said something interesting yesterday, I thought you might want to hear it. Comrade Heym?"

I stood up, wondering whether to introduce myself, and if so whether to use my own name or to go along with Kühn's nominal delusion.

"Oh, sit down, man!" Kühn snapped.

So I sat down and repeated what I'd said to Kühn the evening before, that Bruno's unexpected arrest, coming as it did immediately after his visit to relatives over here, indicated that it probably had nothing to do with his defection, but had been planned by the West German authorities before he went on leave.

The captain moved his lips a little, but no sound came. The new major was looking at his peer, his brow creased and one corner of his mouth hooked in a sneer. By my side, the first lieutenant hadn't bothered nodding while I was speaking, he was studying me as if he'd only just noticed my presence. I returned the favour, and we both looked each other up and down, our faces expressionless.

"We've already discussed this possibility." The blond major turned to Kühn, who was steadfastly admiring the dull view through his window. "It's nothing more than a theory, we can't shut down an operational process on the basis of a vague idea that's not backed up by any evidence."

Great, I thought to myself. *Why did I open my big gob last night? Now I'm being used as ammunition in a battle between two majors.* It wasn't an unfamiliar experience, and I remained silent, waiting to see who would win this round.

"I'm not suggesting we close the files. On the contrary, I'm suggesting we maintain operational ability," Major Kühn made his case, still staring out of the window.

The first lieutenant watched Kühn, but this time he didn't nod along.

"I intend to send the comrade second lieutenant to

interview PKE and customs staff at the border station, see what he can pick up," Kühn said, his gaze settling on me. The other major and the first lieutenant also directed their attention towards me.

"Well, I'll trust your judgement, Comrade Major Kühn," said the blond major. "I believe we've finished here, unless there are any queries?"

We three junior officers stood up and simultaneously reassured the majors that we had no questions.

"Comrade Heym, a moment if you will," Kühn stopped me as I filed out.

I waited by the doorway, back straight, thumbs pressed to seams, ignoring the final exchange between the two majors.

"I hope you know what you're doing," said the blond major as he left.

Kühn didn't bother answering but pointedly looked the other way as the door was shut.

"So now you know how the land lies," Kühn said as he gestured to the table.

I didn't answer, but took my seat again, opposite Kühn.

"Comrade Major, permission to speak?"

The major nodded slowly, and I asked him who the other three officers were.

"You wanted to meet the interrogators, the ones who questioned Bruno." He nodded towards the door. "Now you have. And you heard me tell them what I want you to do next: talk to the Pass and Control Unit at the border station. You may not find anything, but we won't know until we try."

I nodded politely, wondering whether that was my dismissal, but the major wasn't quite done.

"When you've finished at Marienborn train station, come back to Berlin and talk to Rear Services. They'll need a day or two to sort out the paperwork but I want you to go to West Germany as soon as your legend is in place."

22
BERLIN LICHTENBERG

I didn't go to Marienborn until after Christmas. Personally, it wouldn't have been a problem for me to travel on the first or second Christmas Day, but a call to the head of the Pass and Control Unit told me that the shift I needed to speak to were on leave until the 27th of December.

As planned, I spent Christmas Eve and Day in my office. There wasn't much to do, Berlin Centre was practically empty, so I put my feet up, watched the portable telly that I'd brought in and ignored the festive cheer that had descended on the capital. Whenever some bright idea occurred to me, I wrote a memo about it and sent it to various offices in the department, just so everyone would know I'd been working.

Tuesday the 27th finally rolled around and, ironically, the best connection to Marienborn was the international express D444, the same service that Bruno had caught to Cologne three weeks earlier. I picked the train up at Schönefeld, and a few minutes before we reached Magdeburg a transport policeman came through the train, pointedly informing all citizens that the next station was the final stop in the GDR. Not technically correct, but the border station, Marienborn, was scheduled as a boarding-only stop. I didn't have the right stamps on my paperwork to stay with the train that far so for the final leg of the journey I would have to join the proletariat on the stopping service.

When I alighted at Magdeburg, I saw the transport cop in his dark uniform mentally counting us as we filed past. I made my way down the steps to the passenger tunnel as the tannoy announced the international express was only for passengers with a valid exit visa.

The local train was made up of a loco and three grimy carriages. It took a whole hour to rattle along the mere forty kilometres of track between Magdeburg and Marienborn, wheezing into every village and hamlet on the way, stopping to let babushkas wearing coats that were heavier than themselves dodder off down the platform, most of them carrying full shopping bags and walking sticks.

Marienborn Station's only concession to Christmas was a raddled spruce in a pot at the end of the platform. Fairy lights had been wound through the branches, but weren't switched on—Christmas was already over, after all. I walked past the Mitropa station buffet and crossed the tracks by the level crossing on the way to the international platform. Colleagues from the Firm, dressed in border guard uniforms, watched from the end of the international connections platform, while real border guards kept an eye on passengers from an inspection bridge above. A comrade barred my way, standing between a grubby orange railing and a glass kiosk.

"*Ausweis* and travel documents, please," he intoned dully, looking over my shoulder to see whether I had come alone.

I introduced myself and fished out my clapperboard, showing him the page that confirmed I was a fully paid up member of the Ministry. The corporal stiffened and saluted, immediately entering the hut and picking up the phone to pass on my request to speak to the head of the Pass and Control Unit.

"You will be taken to the Head of PKE without delay, Comrade Second Lieutenant," he reported on return.

It was a miserable day, the railings were slick with ice, the stone-grey clouds hung almost as low as the platform canopy and every so often a spit of frozen rain targetted the gap between my collar and neck. I pulled my anorak closer around me and swore at the corporal who'd gone back into his little shelter without inviting me in. Through the window I could see him sitting in the warmth, filling in a grey form at his desk.

An *Unteroffizier* rescued me from the wind and the sleet, and we marched down the platform until we reached an office tucked away in the far corner.

Behind a desk that was big enough to play ping-pong on, a major was staring at a couple of clipboards, each with a form tucked inside a plastic pocket, numbers filled in with felt-tip marker. He handed the clipboards and a couple of felt-tip markers to the *Uffzi*, who rapped out a quick *Sie gestatten, ich melde mich ab, Genossse Major?* and left the room without waiting for permission.

"Two coffees!" the major shouted at the closing door before turning his attention to me. "How can I help you, Comrade Second Lieutenant?" He gestured at the chair on my side of the desk.

I sat down and pulled out my notebook and pen.

"It concerns a passenger who exited the GDR via this border crossing point on the third of December on the D444 express service to Cologne, Comrade Major."

"The paperwork will have been filed with Magdeburg and Berlin by now." The officer frowned.

"I've seen the paperwork," I paused for a moment, enjoying his discomfort. "And Berlin has no concerns in regards to your platoon's efficiency nor the conscientious fulfilment of your socialist duty."

The major's shoulders relaxed as his back softened.

"I would like to speak to those members of the Pass and Control Unit who checked the passengers on that train," I continued.

"You're familiar with the process? Two teams, each beginning at the end, working through the train until they meet in the middle. Each team is made up of a member of the

PKE and a member of the Customs Administration"

I was familiar with the process, but Bruno had been sitting at the centre of the train so either team could have got to him first.

"I'll need to speak to all PKE personnel who had any contact with passengers on that service, and, if possible, the customs officers, too."

"You'll have to speak to Chief GZA about seeing the customs officers. I'll ask the Duty Officer Border Troops to put you in touch."

I nodded, my purpose had been to inform the Head of PKE of my intentions, not to ask for advice, but he wasn't to know that I'd spent years monitoring the smooth running of border crossings into West Berlin.

A stiff silence descended, broken only by the return of the *Uffzi* with two cups and a jug of coffee.

"Pull the records for the third of December," the major glanced at me for confirmation that he had the right date. "And send for the personnel that were on the train that day."

The sergeant nodded and left again, this time without any formality. Wish the CO during my basic military service had been this lenient.

I sipped my coffee—it was good stuff: *Seized contraband*, murmured the major into his cup while he stared at the wisps of smoke that were escaping from the badly fitted iron stove in the corner. The whole room stank of brown coal, auburn ash hung in the air and settled on the cracked lino.

My observations were interrupted by a knock at the door. The major ignored it, and a couple of minutes later there was another knock, followed by the appearance of the sergeant's head.

"Both together or singly, Comrade Major?" he asked.

The major raised an eyebrow in my direction, and I addressed the *Uffzi* directly. "Bring them both in, Comrade Sergeant."

The two men filed in and stood at attention in the corner, casting nervous glances at the *Uffzi* standing beside them.

"May I, Comrade Major?" I asked.

"Go ahead, Comrade Second Lieutenant."

I scraped my chair around so I could see the three soldiers. I wasn't sure of the operational protocol of doing interviews in the presence of the commanding officer and his assistant, but since the major had made no signs of leaving, I decided I had no choice but to press on and hope he would restrict himself to drinking his coffee and staring at the stove.

The sergeant had somehow made it across the room without my noticing that he'd moved. He was now standing beside the major, literally distancing himself from the men I was about to interrogate.

The taller one was a simple soldier, still in his teens, barely begun shaving. The other was a corporal, looking older and more experienced than his comrade, but also obviously not a lifer. They were in winter field uniform and had presumably been pulled from one of the sentry posts on and around the station.

"Comrades, were you in service on the D444 express train to Cologne on the third of December this year?"

After a moment's pause for thought, I got a simultaneous report from both of them: *Jawohl, Genosse Unterleutnant.*

"Which of you began at the rear of the train?"

The young soldier took a step forward. I showed him a picture of Holger and asked if he recognised him.

"Comrade Second Lieutenant," he began doubtfully. "It was three weeks ago, but I believe that person was on the train."

"Tell me."

"He was in possession of West German papers, but was wearing what I considered to be clothing produced in the GDR. Close inspection of his passport, *Ausweis* and other pieces of identification turned up no further inconsistencies, so I moved on."

"Did you report your suspicions, Comrade?"

Behind me, I heard the major mumble something, whether to himself or to his assistant, I couldn't tell. I ignored him, and passed another three photographs to the men in front of me. The two babysitters and Bruno himself.

Neither recognised the two babysitters, but the corporal squinted at the photograph of Bruno for a moment or two.

"Comrade Second Lieutenant," he began, as hesitant as his colleague had been. I made an impatient gesture with my hand and he gathered his wits. "I can't be certain, but if this was him ... I believe, at the time, I was paying more attention to another passenger in his carriage."

The corporal was beginning to sweat beneath his fleece *Bärenvotze* hat. He shoved the photograph at his colleague. "You remember the woman we took off the train?" he asked.

I cleared my throat and the corporal turned back to me, straightening his back even further and blushing as he did so.

"Apologies, Comrade Second Lieutenant. It is possible that the person in the photograph was in the same compartment as a colleague."

"Colleague?" I asked, my interest sharpening.

"She identified herself as a member of the Ministry for State Security and left the train."

I turned to the major who was sharing a sideways glance with the assistant.

"You didn't think to tell me of this, Comrade Major?"

"You didn't ask, Comrade Second Lieutenant," he replied, his voice flat with disdain.

23
BERLIN LICHTENBERG

I didn't get back to Berlin until after ten that night. The train brought me to Karlshorst and I caught the S-Bahn to Frankfurter Allee, walking from there down the slick streets to Berlin Centre.

Major Kühn was waiting for me in his office. I'd called him from a public payphone in Magdeburg, asking for an urgent meeting, but it was an open line so I couldn't tell him what I'd just found out.

"Sit down to give your report, Comrade Second Lieutenant," he said as I came in.

I'd had the whole journey, and several hours waiting for a connection at Brandenburg Main Station to consider how best to make my report. The facts of the situation were clear enough: I'd gone to Marienborn, been told that a female operative had been removed from the same compartment Bruno had been travelling in. The Head of PKE in Marienborn had refused to tell me what had happened to the operative, or let me look at the report.

The incident opened up a completely new aspect to Bruno's journey, but what bothered me more was that somebody in this building had already known about events at Marienborn that day, they'd read the report and filed it. Had Major Kühn known about this before he sent me to talk to the PKE?

It was hard to read anything into the major's manner: his eyes were so far beneath his heavy beetle brow that it was impossible to interpret any emotion; his eyebrows were slightly raised, perhaps in mild interest.

So in the absence of any reason not to, I gave him the full story.

By the time I'd finished my short report, Kühn hadn't rearranged any of his impenetrable features. If I'd been hoping for tell-tale signs, reactions that might have given away what the major knew then I was out of luck. The guileless don't advance to become a major of the MfS.

"Well, well, Comrade Second Lieutenant, you really have uncovered something." The major began tapping his fingers on the table, one digit drumming after another in a repetitive, descending scale.

After a minute or two of admiring his own musical talents, Kühn spoke again. "Leave this with me."

A flick of the chin told me I could go. I stood up, clicked my heels and headed for the door, wondering whether the matter of the unknown female operative had also been dismissed, or whether I could trust the major to find out what had happened to the missing report.

"Progress report from Bonn by Friday, Comrade Second Lieutenant," the major called as I reached the door.

I hesitated in the corridor outside Kühn's office, wondering whether to go and book a train ticket to Bonn right now. The major wanted a report by Friday, and looking at my watch, I could see it was nearly Wednesday, which didn't give me much time to get over there and do my initial scouting around.

On the other hand, I wouldn't make any friends by going to the travel section shortly before midnight—they don't appreciate interruptions at any time of the day and the night staff are particularly fond of their snoozes. I decided to leave them until morning. You never knew when you'd need the travel section staff on your side.

It had been a long day, most of it spent travelling or waiting for connections at stations, and I was restless with unspent frustration. A bar would have been the obvious choice, but only the seediest and most squalid dive would be open at this time of night, and only then if they recognised your face.

I knew a few places that fulfilled the criteria, but I needed to stretch my legs. And there was a question or two I had for Holger before I went to West Germany.

I didn't have my MZ motorbike or my Trabant with me at the Centre and the tram didn't run this late at night, so I started walking northwards, towards Weissensee. There was little traffic on the roads and I heard the Ikarus bus as it drummed up the hill behind me. I was coming up to the crossroads with Lenin Allee, the bus stop on the far side of the intersection—too far to bother making a dash for it—so I watched the bendy bus wheeze past, exhaust condensing on the frigid night air.

I was almost half-way there anyway, so I put my head down and held my hat against the wind while I trudged on.

Ilona took her time answering the door, and when she did, she pulled her dressing gown close around her, hiding the lacy nightdress that peeked through her gaping gown. I began to wonder whether I'd come all this way in the hope that Holger might not be home.

She took one look at me, shook her head and disappeared from sight, leaving the street door ajar. I pushed it further open and followed her up the stairs to their flat. When I got there, Ilona was no longer to be seen. The flat door was pushed to but not shut, so I nudged it open and went into the lit hallway, waiting to see what would happen next.

Holger came out of the bedroom, blinking and running his fingers through his hair.

"Reim?" he croaked.

"I need to ask you something."

"Work?"

I gave him a nod.

"Official questions?"

79

An odd thing to ask, I thought as I watched him rub his face. He was looking more awake now, but still not quite with it. He pulled the bedroom door shut behind him, and with a glance at his son's door, also shut, he ushered me into the kitchen.

"Can it not wait?" he wanted to know.

"Just a couple of questions, five minutes."

Holger pulled a glass off the shelf and filled it with tap water. He took a sip, watching me over the rim. Then he perched himself on the work surface.

"I'm going to Bonn tomorrow morning and there's something that has been bothering me—thought you could help. Bruno said the mole was one of the interrogators?"

Holger nodded again, wondering why this was important enough to wake him in the middle of the night.

"Did he say anything else? Any clues about the identity of the mole? Anything you might have thought of since we last spoke?"

Holger shook his head, no hesitation, no need to think. "I told you all this-"

"Yes, but it still doesn't make much sense to me. Bruno's work involved tracking Red Army Fraction members, so how would he recognise a mole at the Ministry? Something like this is completely outside his field."

I poured myself a glass of water but didn't drink it, just held it while keeping an eye on Holger. He was sleepy and irritated.

"And he told you nothing, no descriptions, no clues? Height, hair colour, fat, thin? Regional accent? Anything? Because right now, I don't believe in your mole."

"Accent?" Holger slapped the base of his hand against his forehead in a parody of remembrance. "Saxon, he said the interrogator was a Saxon."

"And you only remember this now?"

"Sorry, it slipped my mind. Bruno mentioned it in the

middle of talking about his work, it wasn't until you mentioned accents ..."

OK, let's give Holger the benefit of the doubt, he's a friend after all. One tiny problem:

"I've met all three interrogators, none of them are Saxons. Two Berliners and one from somewhere up north. No-one from Saxony, not even a Thuringian among them. You sure you remembered right?"

Holger sipped his water a bit more and rubbed his eyes. "Yeah, I'm sure," he said.

"What exactly did he say?"

"*Der Sachse, der ist es.*"

That was pretty clear, no room for doubt: *the Saxon, it's him.*

24
MARIENBORN BORDER
CROSSING POINT (RAIL)

The next afternoon I was sitting on the international express to Cologne, waiting for the border controls at Marienborn station. I'd picked up my travel documents and train tickets at Berlin Centre and was wearing the West German blue tweed jacket, pink shirt, blue tie and blue poly-mix trousers provided by the department.

This time, because I had an exit visa and was travelling into West Germany, I didn't have to leave the train at Magdeburg, but remained in my seat, in the same compartment in which Bruno had sat a few weeks before.

From the window, I could see border guards along the tracks and as we pulled into the station, I spotted a sentry post on top of the signal box.

The comrades from my old department—the ones wearing the green Border Troops uniforms so that travellers didn't realise they were dealing with the Stasi—were on the platform, making sure there were no unauthorised attempts to board the train. A *Feldwebel* walked past, his eyes scanning the edge of the platform. His dog would be running along the tracks beneath me right now, sniffing for stowaways clinging to axles.

With a clatter of carriage doors and the tramp of heavy feet, passport control and customs entered my part of the train. I could hear compartment doors scraping open, the polite but stern greeting from the customs officers: *Guten Tag, Zoll-*

verwaltung der DDR, echoing down the corridor.

Passport control were already hauling the door to my compartment open. The corporal I'd interviewed just the day before stepped in. The other passengers, a couple of pensioners from our side, visibly shrank at the sight at him. They held out their bluepassports, the statistics forms folded up inside.

Without even a glance at me, the corporal opened up the briefcase hanging in front of his chest to make a flat surface to hold the passports open on. His eyes darted between faces and passport photos, noting the shape of mouth, nose, eyebrows, cheekbones then spending more time on the ear than any of the other facial features. Satisfied with the biometrics, the corporal, in the same stern tone as before, asked the purpose of the veterans' journey.

"Our granddaughter's wedding," the old lady mumbled, looking down. Her husband took her hand and flicked quick glances at the corporal.

The rubber exit stamp was pressed down on the passports and, with a salute, the corporal handed them back.

It was my turn to be checked. I looked into the corporal's eyes, but saw no flicker of recognition. He followed the same procedure as with the old couple, carefully checking my West German passport and my East German exit visa, but didn't bother asking the purpose of my journey.

With a salute and a cursory "Hope you enjoyed your stay in the German Democratic Republic," the corporal was gone.

After a brief visit by the customs officer, who threw an uninterested look into the couple's luggage but ignored me, silence descended in the compartment. There was no murmur of conversation, just the restless shuffle of nervous movements.

I remained in my seat, watching the platform through the window. I felt the judder as train doors slammed shut, and a moment later, the station emptied of life. With a jerk, the locomotive pulled us out of Marienborn, under the inspection bridge and over the level crossing, gaining speed as it entered a corridor of high fences.

Six kilometres later we passed beneath another inspection bridge then the fences abruptly ended. We had reached the West.

I could see the reflection of the old couple in the window, I saw their eyes fall away from the scenery outside, the old man stood up and fetched his bag from the luggage rack, pulled out a wrap of sandwiches and a couple of apples. Another movement yielded a flask.

"Cup of coffee, young man?" enquired the old lady, holding out a steaming plastic cup.

I shook my head. My ears picked up the bustle and hum of conversation—even the odd laugh—from up and down the carriage as the passengers collectively began to breathe again.

We reached Helmstedt a few minutes later and the West German BGS and Customs boarded. Customs took my luggage apart, not that there was much in there for them to look at: some Western clothes and underwear, all from C&A or H&M with a few Karstadt and Horten labels on show for the sake of variety, along with shaving tackle and other toiletries. A sheaf of business papers, impenetrable to all but the most financially-gifted, and an introductory letter beneath a convincingly faked letterhead from the Federal Ministry of Intra-German relations complemented my fake West German identity documents and provided a reason for the ostensible trip to the East.

The papers were ignored but the customs officer was gleefully smug when he came across a half-smoked packet of untaxed Marlboro, bought from the *Intershop*.

I listened to his lecture on how duty-free purchases from *over there* supported the *Ostzone*, that the proceeds from the sales paid for the inhumane and murderous border we'd just passed through. I set my face to politely neutral and pretended to listen carefully as he told me I should really be given an on-the-spot fine for smuggling, but that he'd let me off this time.

After a further minute of desultory searching, the customs officer withdrew, and it was my turn to begin breathing again. The Marlboro had been a deliberate plant, I'd been told the West Germans generally paid more attention to working-age travellers who'd been in the East, and an innocuous packet of coffin nails for customs to confiscate and smoke themselves was far less conspicuous than being completely clean.

The pensioners had watched the set piece with interest, and now the old man piped up: "Sometimes take their job too seriously, don't they?"

I came up with some inconsequential reply and moved to another compartment at the next stop. Didn't need a pair of old gasbags rabbiting on for the rest of my journey.

25
WEST GERMANY
Cologne

It was already dark by the time we neared Cologne. The train crawled across the heavy steel bridge that spans the Rhine and slipped to an untidy halt next to a statue of one of the Hohenzollerns on a horse. I bent low to see the tips of the floodlit cathedral towers through the window. It was the first time I'd been to West Germany, and maybe that was why I saw revisionist symbolism everywhere, starting with these two great edifices: the monumental bridge, dedicated to the Kaiser's family, and the lofty Gothic pile built for a dead religion.

I'd done my preparations well, checked the training films back at the Centre, examined photographs of the station and maps of the city, so when we finally pulled up at the platform, I didn't need to stop to read signs or ask the way, but headed down the steps and under the tracks to the main station entrance. Despite the late hour, the concourse—all glass and red-brick—was alive with travellers and porters, a queue waited patiently outside the late-opening post-office, gangs of teenagers gathered by the left-luggage lockers to drink weak beer and harass homeless drunks who were rolling out their blankets for the night.

Outside, a police car waited in the taxi ranks and rafts of travellers, lit by a neon advertisement for Kölsch beer, waded across the busy square. My confident step broke for a moment as I paused to appreciate the cathedral I'd just been mentally criticising—the intricate tracing of its towers reached high above the station's grimy glass canopy.

A jolt in the back as a man in a trilby and grey overcoat pushed past and I was on the move again, heading for the steps to the tunnel where the trams run. On the platform, I looked around—there were simply too many people here, too many lines serving the station, it was practically impossible to spot any tails. Rather than waste time watching the ebb and flow of the crowds, I took the first tram that arrived, getting off a few stops later, at Poststrasse.

There were far fewer people at that station, and after a couple more trams had gone by, I was the only person left. I boarded the next service and remained standing near the entrance. As the doors began to concertina shut, I squeezed through, back onto the platform, turning to watch as the tram pulled away. I was alone again, just how I like it.

Satisfied with progress, I changed to the opposite platform, catching the next tram to Neumarkt before changing onto a line that ran above ground. One stop later, I left the tram again.

I was now at the edge of Cologne's night life, and without looking around, I dived into the alleyways that lead down to the Rhine, past brightly lit raucous bars and drunken guests who were still imbibing a late Christmas spirit. I turned into a tight lane, finding a doorway to tuck myself into as I watched the way I'd just come. After a couple of minutes I was satisfied I had no shadows and, still in the shelter of the doorway, I changed my hat and turned my reversible jacket inside out to show a darker colour.

Further down the alley, I found an open gate that took me into the back yard of a pub. Keeping my head down, and deliberately swaying a little from side to side, as if I'd been on the beer all night, I went through the back door and into the bar, threading my way through lines of drinkers, arms hooked together, already practising carnival songs. Out the front door,

I darted into another ginnel that beckoned from the other side of the street.

This time, when I found the back door to a bar I had to dodge around a wide barman shouting at me in the incomprehensible sing-song local dialect. I ducked below his outstretched arms, and zig-zagged through the bar, ignoring the curses and names he threw at me.

Back on the lane outside, I had no clear idea where I was, but I headed in a straight line for a few hundred metres, then took a left, down to the river. Sooner or later, I'd hit the banks of the Rhine, from there I'd go downstream, back towards the railway bridge where I'd find a bar on a back alley. That was the rendezvous point with one of our informants.

A middle-aged man was having difficulty balancing on his tall stool. His top button was undone, the grey tie dangling in a puddle of beer on the bar. With a copy of the local tabloid newspaper, *Express*, by his side and a small glass of beer in front of him, he fitted the description I had for my contact.

Pushing my way through the crowd, I sidled close enough to read the date on the masthead of the newspaper. It was from the day before, the 27th of December 1983.

"Yesterday's news is always more interesting," I told the owner.

He turned to look at me, revealing a wide chest and wider belly stretching his shirt. His hair and moustache were slicked back with oil, and a long, thin cigar was stuck into an even longer and thinner face. "You wanna buy it?" he asked in high German tinted with soft Rhenish.

"I've only got Dutch Guilder," I gave him the second part of the pass phrase.

We were interrupted by the bartender who put a narrow glass of beer in front of me. I looked at it, the beer was light with hardly any head and the glass only held enough for a couple of gulps.

"*Wells do gleisch berappe? Ov leever hingerdren*?" the barman asked in the sing-song accent of the city. He held a carpenters pencil in one hand and a beermat in the other.

I had no idea what he was saying and could do nothing better than gawp at him.

"*Gleisch*," said my contact, pushing a five Mark coin over the counter. "*Hä bezahle doch gleisch, un isch met.*"

The barman took the money and slapped a few coins of change down before going back to draw more beer.

"I don't like Beatrix, it's high time she abdicated," said my contact, using high German again. "That's what you needed to hear, no? So now we're both satisfied that we're in good company you can finish your beer and we'll get going."

26
WEST GERMANY
Cologne

We headed along the bank of the Rhine, passing several landing stages occupied by Köln-Düsseldorfer river cruisers, finally reaching a jetty opposite a large white church, its high tower shrouded in scaffolding. My contact opened a gate to let us onto the pier.

I waited while he locked up, then followed him down to a small launch at the end of a landing stage. The boat was made of fibreglass, colour unknown and unknowable in the shadows. I can tell you it was small, just four metres or so in length, similar in size and shape to the Anka angling dinghies so popular at home. A medium-sized outboard motor hung off the transom.

"Get the lines," my contact instructed as he juggled with the choke and pulled the starter cord.

We zipped around the berthed tourist boats and onto the misty river, keeping to the left bank until we'd passed under a bridge. There was still traffic on the water, long lines of barges pushed by tugs with deep fog-horns and deeper draughts that dragged us close as we skirted their sterns.

The gurgle of water lapping on hulls and the beating of engines came at us from all sides, acoustic shrapnel splintering the fog. Our navigation lights were unlit, even though visibility was near-zero on the river, but my contact seemed to know what he was doing. he pulled the rudder hard and we listed heavily as the bow veered towards the far bank.

I clamped both hands on the gunwale, startled by the heavy pitch as we nudged through the wake of a push tug, its three white navigation lights high above us. Within another minute we were in calmer waters, nearing a quay below a suspension bridge, the lights of the convoys out of sight beyond a spit of land that sheltered the harbour entrance.

"Up the stairs. A grey Renault is waiting for you," my contact said, using the engine to hold us against a flight of concrete steps that led to the promenade above.

I stepped off the boat, and the launch scurried astern, back into the dank night. The eddies it left behind were soon swept downstream in the relentless current of the Rhine.

The steps were damp and slippery with slime, the handrail scaled with rust. I paused as I came level with the road at the top of the embankment. As promised, a grey Renault 30 waited, but in the shadow of the bridge, it was impossible to tell whether anyone was behind the wheel. A brief look around, no-one was loitering, so I climbed the last few steps and crept warily towards the car.

There was a driver behind the wheel and she wound down the window as I came close.

"Cold this time of year." Her voice was hard on the frost-bitten air.

"I dislike hot summers," I replied.

"Let's hope spring comes soon."

I walked around to the passenger side and got in. "I don't know who makes these exchanges up, but they never sound anything but stupid," I said as I slid the seat back a couple of notches to give myself some leg room.

"I'm to take you to Bonn." The driver turned the ignition. ingnoring my attempt at small-talk. "I'll brief you on the way."

"Any new developments?"

"Source Bruno was released this morning," she replied. "Right now, he's watching television at home."

★

We were soon on the motorway, heading south. Traffic was light, and my driver made the most of the empty Autobahn, zipping between lorries and fast night-time drivers.

"Far as we can tell, he's under house-arrest," the driver told me. *Sanderling* was the codename she was using. "There's a car parked outside his flat with two men in civilian clothing. They took up position before he arrived home and the car hasn't moved since, although the watchers have changed shift twice."

"Police?"

"We think so. The car is registered to a civilian address, but that doesn't mean much."

Bruno had been brought by car in the mid-morning when Sanderling and her crew had observed him enter his apartment block. His transport had left once he'd entered the building, leaving behind the other car with the watchers. Since then, Bruno hadn't left the building.

There had been no reports in the media, and no news from other sources we keep in the various security and police agencies of West Germany. It wasn't Sanderling's job to interpret the information she was gathering, but she was clearly puzzled by the Bruno situation.

"Any other watchers? Other vehicles, observation from nearby positions?"

"We're working on it. We have our own stationary observation diagonally opposite Bruno's building. It's an empty shop with a good view of his flat. So far we've seen no interaction between the two watchers in the car and any other persons. Our guess is there are no other observation points, just the vehicle."

I waited while Sanderling curved around the motorway junction Bonn-Nord, then told her what I wanted:

"I need you to arrange a diversion—I want to speak to Bruno."

27
WEST GERMANY
Bonn

We drove through Bonn, the motorway first arcing high over railway tracks and industrial estates then ploughing through a housing estate and finally entering the forest. Ten minutes later we entered Meckenheim on the trunk road.

"Federal Crime Agency is that way, best to avoid that neighbourhood if you can. Too many eyes," Sanderling said, pointing off to the right. "Bruno's residence is just to the south of here."

We took a few left turns, the roads growing quiet and residential. Tangles of streets were lined with modern blocks of flats and small shops. Off to the side, small, self-build houses were set in winter-bare gardens.

We pulled up at the side of the road, and Sanderling took me down a narrow service alley, between skips and large wheely bins. She knocked softly on a back door, then used a key to let herself in, holding the door open for me to follow.

The room beyond was dark, and remained that way until Sanderling had shut the door. She tapped a switch and light flooded the empty store-room. That was when I got my first proper sight of her. She looked West German—at ease in her tailored power shoulders and coiffed blonde hair. She was tall, almost as tall as me—which isn't saying much, but gives you an idea of what I'm talking about—and thin: her face was so sharp she could have opened letters with her cheekbones.

Without a word, she took me through another couple of

doors and into the empty shopfront. The only light was from the streetlamps, leaching through the layer of whitewash that had been smeared over the tall windows. Abandoned shelves stood around, and a broken office chair kneeled against the wall.

A diminutive goon sat by one of the windows, his eyes trained on gaps in the whitewash.

"Anything new?" Sanderling asked him.

Without allowing his eyes to stray from the window, the small man held out his notebook and shook his head.

My contact looked at the jottings and gave the notebook back, then beckoned me over to another part of the window.

"Bruno lives in the building opposite, first floor, right hand side." She stepped aside to give me access to a flaw in the whitewash. Through the gap I could see a modern concrete building, each floor set back further than the one below, giving each storey enough space for a stepped balcony. "The observation vehicle is down there, on the bend, facing the other way. And that service road, over there," she pointed out an alley two buildings further on from Bruno's flat, "it leads to the back entrance of the flats. There's a fire door in the basement of Bruno's building, no lock, it's operated by a push-bar and can't be opened from outside."

"Any other way in?" I asked.

"Just the front door."

The watchers in the car were well positioned. Nobody could get in or out of the main door without being seen by them. The back door would have been more promising—the watchers would have to twist round in their seats to keep the mouth of the service road in sight. Shame it could only be opened from the inside.

On the far side of Bruno's building was a detached house in a garden scattered with fruit trees.

"You said you could arrange a diversion?" I checked.

"When were you thinking?"

"Round about now would be good," I replied, watching the flickering blue light in Bruno's window. "He's still up, watching television, seems like as good a time as any."

We synced our watches and agreed Time X would be in ten minutes then I let myself out of the back door of the shop.

It took a few minutes to walk around the block, and a further couple of minutes to survey the garden next to Bruno's building. It was on a bend, the far end out of sight of the watchers' car, and that's where I jumped the decorative palisade fence that divided the garden from the road. It was only a metre high, just tall enough to cast the shadow I needed to work my way along to the trees next to Bruno's building without being spotted.

I was hoping for a handy fruit tree with low branches, something to give me a leg up to Bruno's first floor balcony, but what I found instead was a galvanised downpipe that drained each balcony on Bruno's building. It stepped down between the levels, alternating between vertical and forty-five degree angles. Much better than a fruit tree.

Crouching in the shade of the fence, I found a gap in the planks wide enough to peer through. The watchers were no more than thirty metres away, I could see them clearly in the light of the streetlamps. One was dozing, the other, the one behind the driving wheel, wasn't even looking in the direction of Bruno's flat. At least he was awake.

I watched the second hand on my watch circle round to Time X, and waited for Sanderling's diversion.

Nothing happened for a few more seconds, then a quiet hum lifted itself out of the background noises of a small town at night. With unexpected suddenness, the hum expanded into the rhythm of a vehicle engine as a red Renault 5 turned the corner. It headed towards us, neither too fast nor too slow, I estimated just over 20 km/h. As it passed the watchers' car, a cracking sound shocked the night. The brake lights of the

Renault shone bright and it came to a halt.

A young man got out and examined his side mirror, then spoke to the watcher who'd climbed out of his car and was examining his own mirror. Their voices carried in the still night, but I couldn't hear what was being said. They'd be talking insurance, the watcher would be trying to persuade the young man to forget about exchanging details, to just move on and not worry about compensation.

The second watcher was still in the car, wide awake now, his attention focussed on Bruno's apartment block, just in case the accident was a diversion. Not so amateurish, after all.

Swearing under my breath, I wondered whether I should still chance climbing the drainpipe, but I had to concede it was a non-starter: one watcher was alert, eyes on Bruno's apartment building, and the other, the one arguing with the Renault driver was facing in my direction. The diversion had failed.

It was time to give up on the plan, return to the shop and plot something new with Sanderling, but while I was still dithering a further movement caught my eye. A white figure floated between the dim street lights. Both watchers had noticed the new entrant to the drama, even though the young Renault driver was still arguing.

The white figure came under the next cone of light, an elderly lady, white night-gown, no shoes or slippers, frizzy white hair coloured by the sodium light. She held her arms straight down, fingers rigid, and with each puff of condensed breath came a high-pitched voice.

She zig-zagged across the street, heading for the second watcher who was getting out of the car to meet this new challenge. When she got close, she stretched her arms out and collapsed.

That was my cue, and without wasting another glance at the brouhaha still unfolding on the street below, I shinned up the drainpipe and slipped over the concrete parapet of Bruno's balcony. Behind me a new discussion had been kindled by the woman's collapse.

But now I was more interested in the silence that was seeping from Bruno's flat. The patio windows were open and the television flickered across the net curtain, but there was no sound. Instead, a smell from beyond the windows reminded me of the Lubyanka cellars on a bad morning.

I crept forward, careful not to be seen above the edge of the balcony, and parted the curtain with my gloved hand. In the flickering of the television I could see a tall male curled up on the floor.

An arm was extended towards the window, the fingers pressed into the palm. One look at the lividity along the edge of the hand told me all I needed to know.

This man was dead.

28
WEST GERMANY
Bonn

I nudged the window wider and put a handkerchief over my mouth and nose against the stench. A table at the corpse's feet was lying on its side, a broken terracotta plant pot and a wilted peace lily splayed across the floor. Strands of partly-digested onion and clumps of grey-green vomit glistened in the light of the muted television. The man's face was pale, except where his head was in contact with the floor. Marbling showed how gravity had caused the blood to pool after his heart had stopped pumping.

Kneeling behind his head and leaning over to see his face, I mentally compared his features to the photographs I'd seen in his file. This was Bruno.

I prodded his fingers, they gave way like heavy rolls of rubber, his jaw was beginning to stiffen but could still be manipulated: postmortem rigidity was beginning to set in, time of death was probably early evening that day. As for cause of death: even though there were no obvious signs of trauma, I was confident about ruling out natural causes.

As fascinating as examining the body was, my thoughts were interrupted by the sound of a car drawing up. I stood beside the net curtain that covered the patio windows, holding it apart to look outside.

A marked police car had pulled up and the officers were getting out, adjusting their caps while they looked up at Bruno's window. The observers were back in their car, no sign of the old lady or the red Renault, they must have resolved the situation while I'd been examining Bruno's body.

But the watchers weren't bothering me right now, I was more interested in the cops who were crossing the street on their way to the front door of the apartment block.

I couldn't leave the way I'd come, through the window and over the balcony—the watchers would be paying even more attention than before. The only way out of here was down the stairwell and through the fire door.

A final look around before I left the scene, making sure I'd left no signs of my presence, hadn't stepped in the vomit or dropped anything. It was during the sweep that I noticed the packet of frozen meat patties, thawing out on the kitchen counter, attracting any flies not already laying their eggs in the vomit on the floor. A frying pan stood on the hob, grease coagulated around the edges. Next to that, a plate with some crumbs and a smear of dried ketchup—Bruno's last meal.

I picked up the damp packet of burgers and let myself out of Bruno's flat, finding myself in a softly-lit corridor. Beige walls, brown carpet, dark wood-effect doors down each side. Pushing through a glass door at the end, holding it so that it didn't make a noise as it swung shut, I found myself on a concrete stairwell. The slapping of feet on steps came from below, and I softly made my way up to the next landing.

I paused there, listening to the cops chatting. A similar high, Rhenish accent as in the bar this evening, completely unintelligible, but what I was really listening out for was the sound of the glass door being opened: a swish, followed by a click as it shut again.

I came back down the stairs and peered around the edge of the door frame. The cops were at Bruno's flat-door, still in knocking-politely mode, although one was sniffing around the door frame. I slipped down to the entry hallway, went down another half-landing to the fire escape door and let myself out.

★

By the time I was back at the observation post in the empty shop, one of the cops was standing in the roadway, next to the patrol car. The lights in Bruno's flat had been turned on, were glaring out into the night, and the shadow of the cop's colleague could be seen moving behind the curtains.

"The observation vehicle has been withdrawn," Sanderling told me.

A fire brigade ambulance drew up opposite, and the back doors opened, disgorging a gurney which was taken into the flats. Our observer at the other window took a note of the activity.

"The subject is dead," I said, keeping my voice low so that only Sanderling would hear. Then, slightly louder: "Have you got a bag for this?" I held out the packet of defrosted meat, already poisoning the close air of the disused shop.

The observer went to the storeroom and came back with a freezer bag. I slipped the package in and sealed it.

"I need to contact Berlin Centre," I told Sanderling, speaking softly again, for her ears only.

She gave me a long look, as if assessing whether I had the authority to make the request, then with another glance at the ambulance in the street outside, she motioned to me to follow her out of the back of the shop.

Twenty minutes later, a heavy, bitter smell forced its way through the car's air vents. It settled in my mouth and set about clogging up my throat.

"It's the sugar refinery," Sanderling told me, using her chin to point to a factory we were passing.

We were entering the outskirts of Euskirchen, a town just to the west of Meckenheim, and the further we drove, the more completely the leaden smell of burning sugar beet coated my throat and nostrils, I had to swallow hard to stop retching.

We rattled over a level crossing and a few hundred metres

later passed under a couple of railway bridges. A right turn at the next crossroads, past a weapons research centre and into a housing estate.

Leaving the car on a quiet road, we walked a couple of blocks then, with a quick check that nobody was on the street, Sanderling opened a garden gate and ushered me through. Down steps and through a cellar door. As soon as the door was closed behind us, she turned the lights on.

There wasn't much in the way of furniture down here, just two bentwood chairs and a desk with a telephone and lamp on it. The place smelt dusty, but even stronger than that, the fumes of the sugar factory hung in the air.

"The line's secure, be as brief as you can," she told me. "Use the same dialling codes as you would in Berlin. I'll wait outside."

She turned the lights off and I heard the door open then close. When I turned the desk lamp on I was by myself.

This was a call no operative likes to make, whichever way I dressed it up, my mission had failed before it had even started.

I sat down and lifted the receiver.

29
WEST GERMANY
Euskirchen

I dialled the number and waited. The line clicked and buzzed but there was no ringing tone, nothing to indicate that my call was being connected. I was about to replace the receiver and try again when a voice came through the handset, clearer than if I'd been phoning from Berlin.

"Night duty," said the voice. It was Holger.

I took the handset away from my ear and stared at it for a moment until professionalism kicked in. I didn't ask what he was doing on the end of a line that started on the western edges of West Germany, somehow passing through the border on the way to Berlin. Instead, in a clear and measured voice, I quoted the codeword Sanderling had given me and listened to the slight delay before Holger answered. He was probably as surprised to hear my voice as I'd been to hear his.

"Subject deceased, estimated time of death four to six hours. Request instructions," I told him once he'd confirmed the code.

"Stand by," came the answer and the line went dead.

When Holger called back, he ordered us to get ourselves to Bad Hersfeld and once there to find a particular phone box. He didn't say it—there was no need to say it—but the only reason to order the whole unit to head for a town near the inner-German border was so they could bring us home.

I left the cellar and found Sanderling sitting on the steps outside. Her eyes held mine while I told her the news. She was quiet for a moment then she suggested we get moving.

"Hersfeld's a few hours away, we need to leave now if we're to make it before daylight.

There was a short diversion back to Meckenheim to order the remaining watcher in the shop to pack up the observation post and follow on with the rest of the team, then Sanderling and I headed south.

We sat in the powerful Renault 30, skipping down the Autobahn towards Koblenz. Sanderling was still in the driver's seat, and where there were speed limits, she was scrupulous in keeping to them, where there were none, she put her foot down, the thrum of the tires winding up to a steady whine as we rolled over the smooth tarmac. The West Germans had roads made for getaways, and we knew how to make use of them.

The radio was on, warbling quietly to itself, barely audible over the hum of the engine and the moaning tires. As we crossed the Rhine north of Koblenz a tune tugged at my memory, its familiarity calling for attention. I looked at the dull glow of the radio dial and tried to recall when I'd last heard it. Moonlight Shadow. About eight or nine weeks ago, playing on a radio smuggled from West Berlin and sold to a young landfill worker with more money than sense. Another lifetime.

"They played that song all summer, I thought I'd go crazy if I heard it one more time." The first words from Sanderling since we'd left her crew behind.

I didn't answer, concentrating instead on picking out the few English words I could understand. It was a sad song, I could hear that much, despite the fast pace of the guitar.

"Maybe she's singing about us," said Sanderling. "It's about being on the run."

I looked out of the window, seeing the flapping canvas sides of the lorries we were overtaking, the chains of headlights in the slow lanes. Mike Oldfield's guitar faded out, seguing into the next song. Finally, something in German, something I could understand: Nena and her 99 balloons.

Sanderling drummed along, her fingers tapping the steering wheel.

She didn't comment on the lyrics—a war precipitated by the innocent release of party balloons—and neither did I. We were in enemy territory and we had a recall notice, that was enough to be thinking about for the moment.

Nena's balloons went the way all songs on the radio go, traffic thinned and the motorway, now down to two lanes in either direction, began to curl around the sides of valleys, steadily climbing up to a plateau. The radio reception fizzled and popped, and I twisted the dial, searching for another station. Some dark New German Wave song came on, ponderous lyrics over slow synthesisers and heavy guitars.

"I'm going to miss this." Sanderling again. Couldn't she be quiet for five minutes? "I know, I'm supposed to say something about the music being degenerate, the political-diversive lyrics ... but I'll still miss it."

The radio lost the signal again and I twisted the volume knob to off. We were going downhill now, picking up speed even as the engine comfortably fired beneath the hood. A junction, Sanderling changed down a gear and we slowed to go round the slip onto another motorway. Blue signs flashed past: Limburg.

"I wonder whether I'll fit in at home," Sanderling took her eyes off the highway, watching me as if I might have an answer she'd want to hear. "I've been over here too long, I've forgotten what it's like back in the Republic."

I met her eye, and we both silently acknowledged that she'd crossed a line. What she'd just said was more intimate than anything whispered in bed, it was the kind of loose talk that would get her into serious trouble back at Berlin Centre—if I reported it.

I agreed with her, she'd been here too long, she'd become

soft. She'd lost the revolutionary rigour that is the core of every Chekist. The Reim of three months ago would have stored away the information, used it to his advantage. That kind of talk doesn't have a shelf-life, it can be brought out of the cupboard whenever the need arose, whether to take her down or to bend her to my will.

But I was no longer the Reim of three months ago. Too much had happened since I'd had my comfortable position as Major Fröhlich's adjutant. I'd fallen into deep holes twice, each time sure I was finished. But the first time I'd been saved by good luck and the second time a KGB major had stepped in. One day he'll come calling, asking for repayment.

And now I was in the middle of an operation that had shattered, threatening to rip away the careful cover I'd erected to hide my involvement in the disappearance of not one, but two majors that I'd worked for.

Sanderling reached out her right hand, groping for the radio and twisting it until static seeped from the speakers. She nudged the tuner until she found reception. More music. Synthesisers again, a male voice slurring meaningless English words, the backers giving the song some badly needed definition.

"*Come Back And Stay*," Sanderling hummed along. "How appropriate."

There was a click in my chest, something had changed. Almost audible, but Sanderling, still crooning to the song, hadn't heard. It was just me, opening up.

"Who sent you over?" I asked, knowing that by engaging in this conversation I was kissing goodbye to the Kompromat she had given me, kissing goodbye to the Reim I thought I was.

She gave me the glance again, the same complicit look we'd shared a kilometre or two back. I wanted her to look away, to watch where we going, to use those eyes to navigate around the convoys of lorries and the Porsche drivers flashing past in a blur of chrome and metallic grey.

"I'm in Main Department II." Same outfit as Holger. That explained why he'd been the officer of the day on the other end of the hotline. "Five years ago, that's when I first got here, it was the year that film, Star Wars, came out—have you heard of it? The queues outside the cinemas went round the block. Made me homesick, I'd join in just so I could pretend I was standing in line for a trolley at the supermarket."

There was silence again, the car followed the tight slip off the motorway and onto a trunk road, the radio signal distorting as we went under a bridge, coming back stronger as we cleared the obstruction. Then Sanderling picked up the conversation again:

"At the beginning, I didn't think I'd last five weeks over here, never mind five years. I thought I'd crack under the pressure and be recalled. But I survived my first mission and was given another, then another. Five years, never knowing when it was going to be the last time."

"I've been having thoughts like that myself, just recently," I replied.

"And now I'm leaving my life behind. My flat, all my possessions, my clothes and jewellery. Friends, lovers. Wonder what'll happen when I get back to Berlin, what they've got lined up for me."

"They'll have something prepared. Cosy office, your own phone, dusty plants." I was trying to be reassuring, I realised. It was ridiculous—when had I ever done reassuring?

"I'm finished, I want out. They've had all they can get—there's no more of me left to give."

"You're never finished, not in this business. You're in it for life. You know that," I answered, not unkindly, but Sanderling put a hand on my arm, quietening me.

Um halb-fünf, hier sind die Nachrichten auf HR3, burbled the radio, excited to be bringing the news in the middle of the night. *Cologne. The condition of a senior officer in the Federal Crime Agency has been described as critical following a*

106

suspected terrorist incident in Bonn last night. At this time there are no indications that there are any other victims. A spokesman from North-Rhine Westphalian police has described the situation as contained. Police are searching for the suspects, a male and a female, who are believed to have left the Bonn area, heading south in a grey Citroën 30.

We sat in silence, watching the motorway unwind in front of us. When the newscaster began to inform us of current and expected temperatures, I switched her off.

"Well, someone's doing their best to make sure we're coming back, so you'd better get used to the idea. Forget the music, forget the nice clothes, the friends and the comfortable life. You're leaving it all behind—we're going East, so stop talking about what you've lost, it's not doing either of us any good."

30
WEST GERMANY
Bad Hersfeld

We left the motorway at the next junction and wound into the hills in search of a clean car. We caught a suitable candidate in our headlights in the second village, a medium-sized Mercedes parked by the side of the road, the nearby houses hiding behind tall hedges.

Sanderling let me out and I cracked the Mercedes's door with no difficulty. Leaning down to pull away the moulding around the steering column, I stripped the wires and touched them together to start the car. The dash lit up, showing I had half a tank of petrol to play with, and with Sanderling following behind, I headed for the nearest town of any size, a dump called Kirchheim. We wiped down the Citroën and left it outside a block of flats.

From there it was just a quarter of an hour down back roads to Bad Hersfeld. It would have been better to muddy the trail by getting rid of the Citroën somewhere further south, but we were already behind schedule.

We found the phone box in the centre of Bad Hersfeld, at the foot of a steep hill dotted with well kept houses and tidy gardens. On the other side of the road, the gloomy street lighting struggled against the deep shadows cast by the field-stone wall that surrounded a ruined monastery.

I dialled the local number from memory, letting it ring twice before hanging up and dialling again. This time I let it ring four times then cut the connection and left the cabin.

Reading the map by the light of a filtered torch, I gave Sanderling directions to a large cemetery on the south-east edge of Hersfeld. At the back gate there was space for a few cars to park, and beyond that a field separated us from the motorway. The roads were quiet, no traffic at all on the Autobahn—it led directly to the border crossing into the GDR at Wartha; all roads heading east were practically dead ends.

I was nervous, not so much about going home but about how long it was taking to get there—it was already after five in the morning, people would soon stir, workers make their way to the early shift and traffic head for the border crossing. I felt exposed, sitting in a car in a town I'd never been to, hadn't done preparation for being in and not knowing what, if any, operational support I could expect if I got into a tight spot.

It was the news bulletin that had disturbed me, the mention of the car we'd been travelling in. My first thought had been that it was our side, leaking just the right amount of information, not so much as to be dangerous, but enough to make sure we'd feel the pressure to come home. But now I had the opportunity to really think about it, I wondered whether the West German watchers in the car outside Bruno's flat had been more awake than I'd given them credit for. Maybe they'd noticed not just the traffic in and out of the empty shop, but the vehicles we were using.

"Perhaps they'll tell us to go through the Border Crossing Point at Wartha," Sanderling said, more to break the silence than for any operational reason. "Just like Günter Guillaume, coming home in a limousine, with luggage in the boot and bunches of flowers in our hands."

I didn't agree, there'd be no hero's welcome waiting for us, not like there had been for the agent who had worked his way up to the very top of Willi Brandt's government before being caught and returned to the GDR after a few years in prison.

"Dark VW Polo approaching from the rear, two occupants,"

Sanderling interrupted my thoughts.

I adjusted the central mirror and watched the Polo pull in behind our car. The driver's door opened and a short but well padded man got out. Sanderling's hand dropped to the map compartment in the door, pulling out one of those new-style Glock pistols. She chambered a round.

Holding the *Wamme* in her right hand, she got out, making sure to keep the pistol behind her body, out of sight of the occupants of the Polo.

Without the benefit of a weapon, I opened my own door and got out, too.

The cold was shocking, heavy frost glistened on the cemetery wall, the short man was pulling his coat tighter around himself, hunching his shoulders to shorten the parts of his neck exposed to the air.

"The night train doesn't leave until shortly before midnight," he said, looking between Sanderling and myself.

"We must have an old timetable," I replied.

Sanderling's hand disappeared into her coat pocket, it emerged a moment later without the Glock.

The man made a sign to the passenger in the Polo, who got out and loped past us without looking our way. He got into our Mercedes and, reaching under the steering column, started the engine.

"Any luggage in that car, anything you want to take with you? If so, you'd better grab it," said Shorty, holding the back door of his Polo open for us. "Get a move on, we've a tight schedule to keep to."

31
WEST GERMANY
20km south-east of Bad Hersfeld

The road snaked around hills and between forests before climbing through half-timbered villages that were pasted to the slopes like model railway scenery. We met nobody on the road and our driver pushed the Polo to its limits, winding through the greenery, darting through settlements before the locals had even noticed our passing.

We were at the very edge of West Germany, an area blighted by the border. Farmhouses had fallen into ruin, villages had been half-abandoned and the roads were little better than field tracks. Then the field tracks narrowed further, the forests thickened until the car couldn't continue.

"This is us." The driver stopped the Polo, had already put it in reverse, ready to leave as soon as we got out. "Carry on down this lane, it zig-zags around a bit, but watch out for a sharp left in about a kilometre. The lane heads north and you leave it there. Follow the hedge along the side of the field, two hundred metres later there's another hedge with a ditch behind it. That's the border. Cross the ditch, you're in forward territory of the GDR." The driver had his eyes glued to the rear-view mirror, checking for other vehicles, but he hadn't finished with the instructions:

"Stay on the territory of the GDR, but follow the ditch for another two hundred metres until you reach the first line of the border defences. You'll be met by uniformed Border Scouts who will take you through the fence. You see anything on this side of the border, any headlights, anyone on foot, hit the dirt. You might have noticed the cops are looking for you, so it's possible the *Bundesgrenzschutz* will also be on the alert. Now, get going!"

He took his foot off the clutch even before we'd got the doors shut, and the Volkswagen slithered into a field entrance before turning to go back the way we'd come.

The air was so crisp it scraped my insides when I breathed. Once the car's rear lights had faded, the only light was from the stars and the crescent moon hanging above the valley to the south. Trees pressed in on the north side and we walked in their shadows, ready to take cover if we heard or saw any movement.

We made slow progress, skidding on the ice in the ruts of the lane, stopping often to listen for vehicles, remaining aware for any patrols by the West German BGS border police. The forest on our left petered out, leaving us on the open side of a ridge.

The sharp turn northwards came soon after and we turned off the lane. We were half-way across the ploughed field when we heard the chopper. I didn't have to say anything to Sanderling, she had her nose pressed in the hard soil before I'd even thought about reacting. We each lay in our own furrow, hoping the low moonlight wouldn't cast long shadows of our prone forms.

The helicopter came from the north, still invisible behind the ridge, then, with a clatter of rotors, it flew almost directly overhead before banking to starboard, following the line of the border. Identification was easy: the open trusswork of the tail was silhouetted for a moment against the moon—an Alouette II light helicopter, used by both the Bundeswehr and the BGS.

We stayed low as the helicopter flew on, not moving until the beating of rotors were far to the south, then, checking our limited horizons, we ran the last hundred metres to the hedge at the far end of the field, stumbling over the frost-hardened earth.

The hedge along the ditch was sparse, branches bare but armed with thorns. I parted some twigs to let Sanderling through, all the time looking over my shoulder towards the lane, keeping an eye out for signs of human activity. If the chopper crew had been using night vision goggles, we'd have shone like coals in a stove and someone would now be on their way to investigate.

Safely through the hedge, Sanderling turned to hold the branches apart for me and we jumped the ditch. A few metres further on, a concrete post, painted in black-red-gold told us we'd made it home.

The going on this side was even rougher, nature had been allowed to return, high tussocks of grass grew between stands of slender birch. But we walked more freely now, less worried about being stopped.

We were edging around a spiky bush and had ended up near the ditch again—so close I could hold my arm out and my fingertips would be in the West. That's when the BGS patrol spoke:

"Not another step."

32
INNER-GERMAN BORDER
Hessen / District Suhl

I froze, only my eyes moving as they tried to penetrate the shadows beyond the hedge.

"You're on East German territory" said the BGS border guard in a Hessian accent. "Come towards me, don't pause, don't look around, just come towards me,

I could make him out now, dark green parka and beret, another man behind him, standing further back with a bulky radio pressed to his ear.

The one who had spoken was holding his hand out, taking care not to come too close to the ditch that marked the border. I could see his face, he had wire spectacles on, his mouth was set in a line below a thin moustache, and if he was surprised to see a man wearing a suit and carrying a briefcase out here on the border then he didn't show it.

I looked around for Sanderling, but she'd disappeared from view. Somehow this fact brought movement to my legs again and without saying a word to the West German border policeman, I stepped away from the ditch.

"Towards me!" The BGS policeman didn't shout, but his voice carried authority. "You're going the wrong way!" He paced me on his side of the ditch, keeping me in sight as best he could when I headed further into the dry, winter vegetation. "You don't want to do this, you really don't—come towards me."

Twigs were crackling under my feet now, I was moving as

swiftly as I could, not caring whether my feet landed in the shadows or in the narrow flecks of moonlight that shone through the lattice of boughs above me.

"Halt!" The shout came from the other direction, from beyond where I'd last seen Sanderling. A Saxon accent. "Border guards of the GDR! Remain where you are—raise your hands!"

The BGS policeman fell back a step or two and shrugged off his rifle, pulling it around and holding it ready. His colleague ran up beside him, still jabbering into the radio.

"Hands up!" came the order again, yet another voice, another Saxon, away to my left.

A shot was fired, directly to the south of me, and to my right the *Westler* raised his G1 rifle, aiming it in the direction of the muzzle flash. His colleague let off a flare.

The landscape splintered into shifting patterns of light as the white flare whined upwards then started its long drift down. At the snapping of a twig, I swung to my left. A border guard, one of ours. His Kalashnikov was lowered and he was taking great care to keep me between himself and the Western BGS.

"Put your hands up and come this way," he ordered.

I raised my right hand high, held the left arm in front of me, the briefcase dangling from the end. The signal rocket was still drifting down, shifting the shadows upwards, it made me feel I was falling forwards.

I could hear one of the Westerners as he gave a running commentary into his radio, but I ignored him, he was on the other side of the ditch, out of reach. Taking care where I was walking, I followed my border guard deeper into the thicket.

We'd gone about fifty yards, our route curving round to the south, presumably to where there was a gate in the fence. The white flare finished its descent but my eyes hadn't adjusted to the darkness yet so I stayed close to the border guard. When he turned to check my progress I could see his face, light against his camouflage jacket and the bushes behind him.

I don't know how far we'd gone, I couldn't hear the BGS any more, perhaps they'd shut up and were just watching us. I was stumbling along, wanting to look over my shoulder, reassure myself they'd stayed on their side of the border. That's when another shot cracked the night.

Not a flare this time but a single rifle discharge followed by a scream that echoed over the valley. Sanderling.

I stopped. I looked around, but Sanderling wasn't in sight, I hadn't seen her since the BGS had turned up.

I was still standing, gawping like an amateur when the border guard tackled me around the legs. As we landed, his rifle swung around, hitting me in the side and making me gasp in pain.

"Keep down!" he whispered sharply, still lying on top of me.

The pair of us lay there like lovers in the woods, listening for movement, waiting for another rifle shot. There was nothing, no further sound from Sanderling.

The border guard rolled off me when the beating rotors of the helicopter crushed the stillness like only a helicopter can. We crawled towards the moon as the noise of the chopper blanketed us, the pitch changing as it landed on the field just a few tens of metres beyond the border. A moment later it took off again, the Westerners behind us shouting information and orders, presumably to reinforcements who had just arrived. They struggled to be heard above the whirling rotors as the chopper hovered overhead.

"Run, follow me!" shouted my guard, holding his rifle in one hand and loping easily across the broken ground, stooping below the hanging branches.

I followed as well as I could, tearing my trousers on brambles and losing my hat along the way. When I got to the gate in the fence it was standing open, two guards beside it and another pair on the other side.

"Where's my colleague?" I demanded.

"Let's get you out of the forward area, Comrade," said one of the guards, putting a hand on my back and firmly pushing me through the gate.

33
VACHA

A *Stoffhund* open-top Trabant jeep was idling on the patrol road, and I was bundled into the back, the engine skirling into life as soon as I hit the seat.

"Where's my colleague?" I shouted to the *Feldwebel* sitting next to me, my voice competing with the shrill engine and the drum of tyres over perforated concrete slabs.

"She's still in forward territory—the Border Scouts are bringing her in." He turned away and pretended to be interested in the fences, the bunkers and the telephone columns that loomed out of and disappeared back into the gloom, as if he'd never seen them before.

We followed the patrol road along a river valley until the border swept away to the left when we stopped to open up a gate in the inner fence. From then on we were on civilian roads, and a yellow sign at the entrance to the small town of Vacha let me know exactly where I was. Through the town, along the side of the cable-works, across a small bridge and past a sentry post before climbing a hill to the Border Company's base.

It was still dark when we arrived, but the barracks were wide awake, the night shift climbing down from LO and W50 trucks that had brought them back from their posts.

The *Stoffhund* pulled up at the main entrance and the sergeant came around the vehicle to stand beside me as I climbed out, indicating I should go up the steps to the company building.

"Operational co-operation with the Ministry for State

Security," he told the UvD, the duty NCO, who was sitting in his cubby hole to the side of the entrance hall. "I'll take him for breakfast, will you inform the colleagues in Administration 2000?"

The night watch were filing past the UvD's office and handing their *Kaschi* rifles into the armoury further down the corridor, but we took the other direction, picking up a couple of trays before queuing at the food counter.

The sergeant still hadn't said anything to me since I'd got into the jeep, he'd confined communications to nods and polite gestures. That was fine, I had no questions the sergeant could answer and, sooner or later, I'd bump into someone from my own Ministry and they'd be able to tell me what the hell was going on.

Besides, the adrenaline rush from the incident at the border had ebbed and now my lack of sleep was catching up with me, so I wasn't feeling chatty. Which is how we ended up sitting opposite each other at a table, munching our breakfast in collegial silence. I picked up a couple of apples and put them in my pocket. Emergency provisions.

I'd finished my bread and sausage, and the *Feldwebel* had taken my mug for a refill of coffee. The food had done me good, but the coffee was doing me better and I'd become restless, wondering when Sanderling would get here.

I was considering a third coffee when a red-faced NCO with a prominent chin marched up to our table. He was wearing the UvD armband, but he wasn't the same duty NCO as before, must have been shift change for him, too.

"Transport for the guest is waiting in the yard," he announced, standing uncomfortably close in an effort to encourage me to get up from the breakfast table and leave his company to their duties.

"And my colleague?" I asked the *Feldwebel*, who had got up from the table and was staring down at me, also hoping to get rid of me sooner rather than later.

He didn't answer, just held out his arm, helpfully pointing me towards the door in case I'd forgotten the way out. I stubbed out my cigarette, drained my coffee, left my tray on the table and did them the favour of leaving.

A sand-yellow Moskvitch with Gera district plates was waiting for me at the side entrance, so I got in.

The driver didn't turn around, and there wasn't much I could tell from the back of his head. Dark hair, military cut. Wide shoulders inside a civilian jacket.

Wanting to know more, I asked him a question:

"What can you tell me?"

If I was hoping for an answer, I'd have been disappointed.

34
JENA

If there's one thing I've learnt in my years at the Firm, it's that it's not worth arguing. Once the brass get an idea into their heads, there's no stopping them. Best just to wait things out.

Deciding I should follow my own advice for a change, and taking comfort in the fact that I was sitting in a chauffeur-driven Moskvitch rather than banged up in a cramped cell in a Barkas, I put my head down and got some shut-eye.

I slept well in the back of the Moskvitch—it's a much quieter and smoother ride than a Trabant—and I didn't wake up until we were turning off the motorway. I saw the sign, Jena, and smiled. Last time I'd been here, it had been spring, my Boss had sent me to liaise with the local Department XX who were planning to wipe out a group of dissidents that were getting too uppity for their own good. Nice bunch of lads down here, they had some interesting ideas about forcing the troublemakers out of the country. My job had been to liaise between the Jena branch of the Firm and the Passport and Control Unit at the rail border crossing point in Probstzella.

Good times—before everything started going wrong for me.

We turned south on the F88, wherever my silent driver was taking me, it couldn't be far—our little Republic ended forty or fifty kilometres further down this road. It was mid-morning now and from the back seat I had a good view of the surroundings—a pretty route, the river Saale to the left, steep, wooded hills to the right. But I'd been here before and I still had some sleep to catch up on.

★

The F88 is a windy road and all the sharp curves meant I didn't get to sleep too well and I was awake when we arrived in Saalfeld.

We crossed the river and the road mounted a second bridge, this time over the railway tracks. To the south-west, the sun was trying to break through the clouds. Frost glinted on some of the lesser used goods lines. Steam trains in the sidings were being heated, their chimneys belching grey-black smoke that shed fine, red grit as it billowed towards us. Behind it all, the Thuringian Slate Mountains massed, a natural rampart along which the border to Bavaria runs.

It was just a blink as the Moskvitch sped over the bridge and out of the town, a snapshot of tangled tracks pointing towards the hills. The steel rails dividing and coming together held some meaning for me and I tried to work out why—but it was like when you wake up after an epic dream and you know you have just a moment to try to work out what it could mean before the whole story slips away from you. Definitely still had some sleep to catch up on.

When the blast furnaces of the Unterwellenborn steelworks came into view, we turned off the main road, the driver taking the car up the valley, along the side of the forest. Patches of dirty snow loitered beneath pine trees, potholes were crusted with frozen mud. Steam and smoke from the plant flattened into layers in the still sky.

My left thigh had gone to sleep and I turned awkwardly on the seat, bumping up against the apples in my jacket pocket.

"How much longer?" I asked, wondering whether it was time to break out the emergency rations.

"Nearly there, Comrade." Even as he said it, he steered into a smaller lane that crossed the contours of the steep slope, worming its way past an unoccupied sentry box and between the trees until a hunting lodge the size of a villa lifted into view, nestled against the wooded slope.

We drew up by the entrance, a suit opened the door and

122

came down the steps. He wasn't in uniform, but he might as well have been. His hair was shorn at the back and sides and his progress across the concrete slabs of the driveway could only be described as marching.

When you look at a member of the armed organs—doesn't matter whether it's People's Police, Border Troops, National People's Army or the Firm—you can put them in a box: soldier, NCO, junior officer, senior officer or cosmonaut. And this was a senior officer, a caterpillar carrier: if he was in uniform he'd be wearing the furry braid shoulder boards of a major or above.

My driver smartly stepped out of the car and stood at attention. With a moment's delay to gather my wits, I did the same.

There was silence as the officer looked me over, and he had something to look at. My Western suit was ruined. Not just crumpled after twenty-four hours of constant wear, but stained with mud and ripped by the brambles and blackthorn bushes at the border. I stank of stale sweat, and going by the length of the fuzz on my tongue, my breath wasn't all roses, either.

35
HUNTING LODGE, SAALFELD

From my window I could see down the valley to the slag heap that divided the steelworks from the eastern edge of Saalfeld. It wasn't the best view ever, but whatever I was here for, it wasn't to admire the scenery.

The major had taken his time inspecting me. When he'd finished a flunky had appeared from the lodge and brought me here.

If I was already confused about what was happening, my confusion grew when I saw the room. It was comfortable enough, a decent breakfast waited for me on the desk by the window and there was a key in the door—on the inside. Those were all good signs, and I knew to appreciate them.

But neatly laid out on the bed were a grey towel, as pliable as cardboard, a blue tracksuit, cheap tartan slippers and grey underwear that made the towel look soft: prisoners' clothes. I'm not a proud man but I wasn't keen to put on that outfit— the last time I'd worn a blue tracksuit was when they had me banged up in Hohenschönhausen prison, interrogating me non-stop for seventy-two hours at a time.

I took the towel and went in search of a shower. It wasn't hard to find, a communal wash room and three toilet cubicles were just down the hall, at the back of the building. A thorough wash followed by a close shave and a brush of the teeth and I was ready to go back to my room. I ignored the clean, dry prison clothes on the bed and took fresh underwear and socks out of my briefcase then put the grubby suit back on.

I stared out of the window and ate my second breakfast.

Where was I? That was easy. On a hill above the road somewhere between Saalfeld and Unterwellenborn.

But what was this building? Pass.

Obviously I'd been expecting a debrief, but why wasn't it taking place at Berlin Centre? If they were in a rush then the MfS District Administration where we crossed the border, in Suhl, would have had suitable facilities. Instead, I'd been brought to a small town in a small district, to a building which clearly wasn't being used for the purposes of administration. A conspirational flat.

And since I was already asking questions: where was Sanderling?

The debrief began half an hour later. The flunky knocked on my door and did the whole clickety-heels thing before inviting me downstairs for a chat.

The major was sitting at an antique oval dining table, eight chairs placed around the edge. Otherwise the huge room was empty, there weren't even any curtains over the tall windows that had a view down what was once a lawn, but was now mainly moss and dead weeds.

Once the flunky had marched off, the major told me to sit down. There were no introductions, he knew who I was but didn't feel the need to let me know who I was dealing with. I should have gone on strike, asked to see some identification so I could be sure he had the necessary authorisation to talk to me. That's what the rules say, but in real life we all know that nobody likes barrack room lawyers. Senior officers least of all.

So I sat down and waited for his questions. But he started with an apology:

"I'm sorry about the limited choice of clothes—the tracksuit was all we could get at short notice."

So that was that little problem cleared up. Nobody had been willing to donate a pair of trousers, a shirt or a jumper and the shops were empty—as always at this time of year: Christmas stock has sold out, and what truck driver wants to do deliveries between Christmas and New Year?

Still didn't mean I was going to put that blue tracksuit on for him.

The major's nose was twitching now, he was wondering whether I'd taken the opportunity of a shower. Perhaps I should have told him the smell wasn't coming from me, but from my briefcase. He didn't ask, but I lifted my bag onto the table and opened it anyway. I pulled out the freezer bag with the carton of burgers. The clear plastic was bloated with fermented gases or whatever it is that rotting meat gives off. Dead flies speckled the bottom of the bag and dying maggots were attempting to crawl out of the cardboard box. It wasn't very pretty.

"Before we start, this needs to go to the nearest lab. Source Bruno had one of these burgers shortly before he died," I said, carefully laying the bag on the table.

There was no need to mention any suspicions I had about the meat being poisoned, the unhappy maggots were testimony to that and the officer got the idea, leaning back in his chair, trying to get as far away from the sample as he could without losing face.

The flunky appeared, no idea how he knew he was wanted. Maybe he followed his nose.

"Get this sample to Operational Technical Sector in Gera for analysis," ordered the major.

The flunky got the drift and took the bag out at the double. A moment later a Wartburg coughed into life and made its way down the driveway, just visible at the end of the moss. I couldn't see who was at the wheel, but was prepared to put a small bet on it being the flunky, which would mean this officer and I were now alone in the big house.

He was on his feet, heading towards the windows to let some of the stink out. That gave me my chance to look him over. Tall and thin, but not gangly. There was still muscle under his shirt, even though he must have been in his mid-fifties. Full head of grey hair, but his regulation moustache was yellowing, whether from tobacco or residual pigmentation I couldn't tell.

But that wasn't all I knew about him. The most interesting thing wasn't what I could see, but what the flunky had said: *Jawohl, Genosse Oberleutnant*, he'd answered after receiving his orders. I was seldom wrong when it came to finding the right box to put members of the armed organs in, but I'd made a mistake here. The man opposite was a first lieutenant, only a couple more pips on his shoulder than I.

That put a whole new perspective on the situation.

Of course, rank isn't everything. I've led operational teams with officers who outranked me. But if you're still a first lieutenant by the age of fifty then you're a jobsworth. You've missed the early chances of promotion, risen through the ranks on the strength of time in service rather than ability. And he wasn't even a very good jobsworth, hadn't even made captain yet.

I didn't like the situation, so I stalled for time.

He was still at the windows, fumbling with a catch when I stuck two fingers down my throat. The results were better than I'd hoped for.

The first lieutenant swivelled around at the sound of my vomiting, backing into the glass. I couldn't see his face, I was still doubled over, concentrating on some convincing retching.

"Poison," I gasped, hawking up a piece of badly-chewed and partly-digested sausage that had stuck in my throat. I staggered to my feet and headed for the doorway.

Once in the hall with the door firmly shut behind me, I straightened up and made for the bathroom to swill my mouth out with water. Hurrying into my bedroom, I stuck my head out of the window and had a good look at the grounds in front of the house. I could see the drive curling down the slope, dense spruce on one side, abandoned lawn on the other. Leaning out, I could see more spruce and pine closing on the house to either side.

What I didn't see was any sign there may be a telephone in the building. Electricity came up the drive on poles, but the ceramic insulators that should hold the telephone lines were empty. Little point tip-toeing around the house looking for the phone, then.

Another lean out of the window to examine the outside of the building. The rendering had flaked away, exposing the brickwork, and the weather had nibbled at the pointing. Tempting as it looked, I knew there was no safe way for me to shimmy down the facade. I was a desk-stud with a side line in operational activities, not a member of the anti-terrorist Unit IX.

Taking the key out of the door and hanging the blue tracksuit jacket over the doorknob to hinder any attempts at peeking through the keyhole, I went out into the hall and locked my door behind me.

In the bathroom, I pulled one of the frosted windows open and looked out at the spruce woods that pressed against the house. The ground was higher on this side, barely a two-metre drop from the windows. But before I let myself out, I had just one minor problem to solve.

Taking the top off one of the toilet cisterns, I waggled the pin in the lift arm until it came loose, then put the lid back on the tank. Back at the window, I took my tie off, held the wide end against the bottom edge of the window and drove the pin hard through the fabric of the tie and into the rotten wood. The pin was too blunt to properly penetrate the material, but the window frame was so rotten that the pin and the end of the tie had ended up deeply embedded in the wood.

I gave the other end of the tie an exploratory tug before climbing out, pulling the window shut behind me as best I could while squatting on the rotten sill and holding onto the side. Making sure the tie was draped over the sill and hanging down, I shuffled around and over the edge, hanging by my fingers for a second or two before dropping the last few centimetres onto the needle-strewn soil under the trees. Reaching up, I pulled the tie until the window was practically closed, anyone looking into the bathroom wouldn't immediately notice my escape route.

A last tug, but the tie remained attached to the window, jammed in the frame. It hung there, obvious to anyone who cared to take a stroll around the perimeter of the building. Nothing I could do about it, so I left it and headed deeper into the woods.

36
SAALFELD GORNDORF

People in Saalfeld gave me strange looks. Couldn't blame them—a stranger wearing a worn and ripped Western suit turns up in an insignificant suburb of their arse-end-of-nowhere town—more than enough reason to take a second look.

Nobody challenged me, and the couple of people I asked for the nearest phone box were polite enough, but somewhere along the way somebody must have reported me. Fucking grass.

I'd paused outside a new-build block, plenty of greenery and trees, pleasant enough, but it didn't match the detailed route instructions the old biddy had given me just a couple of blocks earlier. According to her, I should now be face to face with the local supermarket and, more importantly, the telephone kiosk by the entrance. Instead, I was looking down a gap between two rows of 1950s slab-built blocks of flats, all set up like dominoes, ready to be knocked over.

"Good morning."

The greeting came from behind me, but I didn't have to turn around to know what kind of person said *Good morning* in that kind of way. And when I turned around, sure enough, there was a policeman, for the moment still at the courteous stage, hand touching his brow in the polite, toy-soldier salute the *Volkspolizei* do. A glance at the patch on his sleeve: *Abschnittsbevollmächtigter*, the beat bull responsible for keeping his beady eye on the local neighbourhood.

"You look a little lost? May I see your papers?" he

continued in his graciously superior way.

And that was my problem. Sure, I had papers: I had a forged West German *Ausweis* and a counterfeit West German driving licence and a sheaf of other official-looking pieces of paper in my jacket pockets. All were pretty realistic, all were in the made-up name of Benjamin Dorn.

What Benjamin Dorn didn't have was a visa for entry into the GDR, nor a stamp to confirm he'd reported to the local police station immediately on arrival, as all citizens of non-socialist countries are obliged to do when they visit us.

Benjamin Dorn was in trouble.

Funnily enough, my training never included anything on the subject of what a Stasi operative should do when copped in the homeland without valid identification. Usually, we've got papers for every occasion, under normal circumstances, I'd whip out some high-status ID card and I'd put this policeman in his place.

Not today.

I was still scratching my head—did I mention I was a bit tired?—when the policeman decided it was time to get shirty with me. "Your papers!"

It was all in the tone of voice. The way he'd said it— arrogant, authoritative—that was familiar. I can do that. In fact, that's what I'm best at.

I leaned forwards and injected so much contempt into my voice that I nearly had to sit down afterwards. "Second Lieutenant Reim of the MfS, based at Berlin Centre. Take me to the nearest police station immediately."

It did the trick. I got another salute and a respectful *Follow me, Comrade*, and he led the way, marching along as if he were at the head of his own personal platoon of the Feliks Dzierzynski Guards.

★

He didn't take me to a cop-shop, but to a bare and windowless room on the ground floor of the cultural centre.

"Gorndorf ABV facility," he announced proudly, standing at the door of the office used for receiving local citizens when they wanted to gossip about neighbours and workmates.

It was poky, barely enough room for the empty desk and a couple of ancient chairs. But I'm not fussy, there was a phone and a door I could shut, I didn't need much else.

Ordering the beat officer to wait outside and make sure I wasn't interrupted (always a good move: give petty officials a task and they'll stay out of your way), I checked the dialling code from here to Berlin and picked up the receiver.

"Officer of the Day, ZAIG," said the voice at the end of the line.

"Second Lieutenant Reim here. Urgent for Comrade Major Kühn, Section II—I'll wait."

And wait I did. And while I hung around, receiver pressed to my ear, I began to have doubts about phoning Kühn. Too much time for thinking, never a good thing. My head was reminding me that superior officers rarely, if ever, appreciated being disturbed, and that's why, when the connection snapped and died, I wasn't annoyed, but actually a bit relieved.

I was about to replace the receiver when it crackled into life again, and the voice of Comrade Ehrlich, Major Kühn's secretary, came down the line.

With some reluctance she put me through to the major, but not without making me wait a further five minutes.

"Kühn speaking." Finally, there he was.

I filled him in on the situation, that I'd returned to the East and was in a conspirational building near Gorndorf in Saalfeld with an unnamed first lieutenant who was keen to debrief me.

"Sit tight, say nothing," the major said. "Give Comrade Ehrlich the address." And with another click and a buzz, I was transferred back to the secretary.

★

Assuming *sit tight* meant I should return to the hunting lodge, I left the policeman's cubby hole and informed him that his assistance was no longer required. I made the mistake of offering a handshake and he blew up with pride, his face turning red with the excitement of having the opportunity to help the Ministry. Finally managing to extricate my hand, I left him stalking around the housing estate, looking for children to intimidate and moped-drivers to check the paperwork of.

By the time I got to the bottom of the lane that led to the lodge, I realized I'd have to give up any thoughts of creeping back in through the bathroom window. Actually I was having second thoughts about the whole returning to the lodge and sitting tight idea—the sentry post at the gates, previously unmanned, now housed not one, but two goons who were developing a serious interest in my approach.

It was when they left their little cabin and spread out to meet me on different trajectories that my second thoughts solidified into action. But I didn't get far, less than a hundred metres down the lane a Lada appeared, and another couple of goons jumped out, blocking my escape route.

37
HUNTING LODGE, SAALFELD

Once they were sure they had the right man, they hustled me indoors, a goon in front, a goon behind and one on either side of me—they really didn't want to take any chances.

I kept my mouth shut, and at least they were polite enough not to give me any of that tough-talk bullshit that we heavies are liable to.

We got to my room and they shoved me in, the door shut and locked from the outside. Looked like I was going to be sitting tight, after all.

I was doing the maths in my head: if Major Kühn was as good as his word and was already pulling the necessary levers then someone from the Ministry's district administration in Gera could be here within a couple of hours. Orders brought directly from Berlin Centre would need about twice that time.

But if Kühn was sitting in his comfy office, smoking a Cuban cigar and pondering the best course of action, deciding how to gain an advantage over whichever department was holding me, then I wouldn't hear from him until tomorrow at the earliest.

I did the maths, then added it all up once again but still came to the same answer. Best case, I'd be out of here by this evening.

I stared at my watch for a bit, looked out the window for a while, and with nothing else to do, I went to sleep.

★

I woke to the sound of a Wartburg engine and, transferring myself from bed to window before I'd even had a chance to rub my eyes, I was in time to see the flunky get out of the car and go to the front door. That brought the total to five men in the building, not including myself and First Lieutenant Jobsworth downstairs.

I smoked my last Western cigarette and, not seeing what I could do about the worsening odds, made the decision to continue trusting that Kühn was still interested in both me and my mission.

The next time I woke, it was because of a key scratching in the lock. The flunky came in, stood at attention just inside the room and informed me that the first lieutenant requested I pack my things and get myself ready to ship out.

I lay back on the bed and crossed my feet.

"You got a cigarette?" I asked, as casually as I knew how. It's not like I was expecting him to smile and pull a packet of f6 from his pocket, but I wasn't in the mood to start packing.

Flunky remained at attention, watching me out of the corner of his eye and plucking at the seam of his trousers.

"Tell me something: I saw you carrying a dispatch bag when you returned from Gera; did it, by any chance, happen to contain orders from Berlin?"

Instead of answering, the Flunky repeated his message, the one about me needing to get ready for a move to a more secret and secure location.

"Tell the Comrade First Lieutenant that I'll pack my toothbrush once he's told me where he's moving me and under what authority he is doing so." I put my head back on the pillow and did my best to ignore my visitor.

It was a relief when he gave up and left—the draught from the open door was giving me a stiff neck.

★

The next visit wasn't so friendly, but I was prepared. After disappointing the flunky I'd searched the room, looking for something I could use to defend myself with. Since I could find none of the usual weapons, I'd no choice but to break the leg off the wooden chair.

They tried to surprise me, but I was waiting for them. I may have been dozing, but I had the chair leg in my right hand, and I had one ear open—listening out for the squeak of loose floorboards on the corridor outside. When the squeal came, I swung my feet off the bed and shook my head to clear the sleep out of it.

By the time the lock scraped open and the handle turned, I was in position. I did my favourite trick—it's surprisingly effective—I waited for the first person to come through the door, leaving enough space for the second to start coming in. You don't need me to tell you what I did with the chair leg, and you probably won't want to hear about how I used the edge of the door as a fulcrum to lever the second man's arm until it cracked.

The third bloke now had two bodies to climb over, one shouting in pain, the other prostate and just generally lying in the way. There was a fourth goon, I could hear him shouting in the corridor, out of sight. Four of them against little old me, and there wasn't much they could do. They couldn't both fit through the door at the same time, not without trampling their friend who was griping on the floor about his broken arm, and that made it hard for them to rush me.

I stood there, legs bent to lower my centre of gravity, swinging the chair leg and looking menacing. Nothing much about this situation was going to change soon, not unless one of the goons got round to remembering their guns.

Judging by the narrowness of their brows, that might take a while.

38
HUNTING LODGE, SAALFELD

There was only so long I could keep the Thuringian stand-off going. I had two angry goons ready to thrash me, and two injured on the floor by my feet. The first one was beginning to show signs of waking up, the other was still groaning and calling for his mama. Sooner or later, he'd realise his arm was broken, not his legs, and he'd wander off, leaving space for the others to come at me. I didn't enjoy seeing his ugly coupon but I still preferred him on the floor, where I could keep an eye on him.

I took another swipe at the two goons in the doorway, the chair leg didn't connect with either of them, but that wasn't the point. I just didn't want them getting any clever ideas.

Except we'd been in this holding pattern for so long that they were starting to get ideas. One of them stepped forward, leaned over the body of his screaming colleague and flicked his truncheon at me. He wasn't trying to hit me, just wanted me to keep my distance—same tactic I'd been using. His baton was longer than my chair leg so he had the tactical advantage. If I wanted to avoid being hit, there was little I could do except fall back a pace or two every time he came at me.

He kept waving his truncheon, forcing me back until his buddy could get close enough to pull the heavy with the broken arm out of the way. The wails of pain were nearly as distracting as the truncheon swishing around my ears, but the way through the door was now clear. The guy I'd hit over the head was still lying there, unfortunately he was far enough inside the room that he wasn't blocking the doorway.

The goon coming at me wasn't as stupid as I'd thought he was—he anticipated the same move as before, the one where I slammed the door in his face, which is why he braced his boot against the bottom of the door, preventing me from swinging it into him. But stretching out to block the door wasn't his wisest move, it put him off balance and when I gave him a hard shove in the chest with the end of the chair leg he windmilled backwards into his colleague's arms.

I hooted as I slammed the door shut, then grabbed the broken chair and jammed it under the handle. That'd keep them out of the way for a couple of minutes.

I crossed the narrow room in two strides and pulled open the window. I'd already checked this out, it wasn't the best escape route ever, but it was the only one I had.

I ignored the way the door was shivering under the impact of blows and shouts from the other side and threw one leg over the window sill. Gripping the frame and bringing my other leg over the ledge, I did exactly what you shouldn't do in situations like this.

I looked down.

And I froze.

I didn't freeze because of vertigo or anything like that. I stopped because I could see a Skoda coming up the drive.

Just what I needed—more goons wanting to join the fun.

The car stopped by the door and, instead of a handful of mindless thugs from the Ministry, it was Holger who stepped out of the beige Skoda. He was wearing his grey, everyday MfS uniform, complete with medal ribbons, and he stood there straightening the seams of his trousers and shooting his cuffs.

"Holger! Get your arse up here!"

I didn't see how Holger reacted to the sight of me hanging out of the window. Before he'd had much of a chance to enjoy the view, the goons had broken down the door and I had the pleasure of joining their unconscious colleague on the floor.

39
BRIESEN

When I came to, I was lying on the back seat of a car going down a motorway. I could tell we were on the motorway because of the rhythmic tock-tock of the wheels as we drove over the expansion joints of the concrete surface. If I wanted to know more than that, I'd have to open my eyes and sit up.

I gave it a go, but it turned out to be a bad idea and I sank back down. My head felt like a T-72 panzer had driven over it.

I tried again. More slowly this time. I got my eyes open far enough to see the back of Holger's head, he was in the driving seat directly in front of me.

Reassured, I close my eyes and concentrated on not puking.

The second time I woke up, it felt like somebody had taken my head off for reconditioning and not bothered screwing it back on properly. It was dark, so opening my eyes no longer meant exposing them to the grey winter sun, although I had to make sure not to look at the glow of headlamps from oncoming vehicles.

"What's the score?" I mumbled over the rattling wheels.

"There you are. Was wondering when you'd join us again." Holger was being jolly. I'd never liked it and right now I liked it less than usual. What I did like was the packet of cigarettes and the matchbox he held out for me, his arm bent back so I could reach the offering between the front seats.

"Tone it down a notch, will you?" I took a cigarette and lit it, ignoring the nausea caused by the movement. "And give it me, words of one syllable or less."

"You've been out of it for a while."

He was telling me things I'd already worked out, and since thinking and listening made my head swell, I wished he'd just get to the point.

"I got there just in time, they were really laying into you. Why do you always have to piss people off so much?"

"Something about being locked up. Brings back bad memories," I answered, trying to sit up in the back seat. I got there in the end, wound the window down and flicked the cigarette out into the night. It had just made me feel worse. I wound the window back up, decided the whole experiment had been a mistake and lay back down again.

"Take it easy, Reim. We'll be there soon."

Be there soon turned out to be three more hours of motorway and another ten or fifteen minutes nosing through solid woodland, down a track made of the same kind of perforated concrete slabs used for patrol roads along the western border. We were driving slowly, but still we had to stop to allow me to vomit, and after that I walked, unable to face the idea of getting back in the juddering car. Holger drove behind me, the Skoda's headlamps lit the way.

On the whole, the walking did me good, I didn't feel so nauseous any more, although the cold air settled around my head like a clamp.

We rounded a corner to find our way barred by a soldier standing in front of a red and white boom. He was wearing winter field uniform, the white piping on his epaulettes indicating motor rifle troops. All very interesting, but I was in no state to guess whether he really was army, or one of ours in disguise.

I stood there, looking at him, and he stood there looking at me, his *Kaschi* slung over his shoulder. Of the two of us, he was definitely the most unsure—I didn't have any energy to waste on that kind of thing.

He remembered his role the moment Holger got out of the car, coming to attention at the sight of my friend's grey uniform jacket.

Holger flicked his clapperboard at the sentry and got back in as the boom rose, allowing us to continue through the chain link perimeter fence and around another sharp curve.

The next gate was set into a high wall, part of which was made up by the backs of low buildings. A lonely light acted as beacon, pulling us in towards the second checkpoint. Holger dipped his hand into his pocket and pulled the clapperboard again.

Once past the second sentry, he parked the car in a courtyard made up on three sides by single-storey outhouses and accommodation blocks, on the far side stood an old forestry building. I'd never been here, but it looked familiar—as if I'd seen pictures of it, or someone had once described it to me. I waited by the car door, and when Holger got out I leant in to whisper:

"Is this Building 74?"

"This is where they held Bruno, yes."

40
BUILDING 74
Sick bay

If it had been up to me, I would have gone straight to bed but they made me report to the sick bay first. The guy in the white coat with the stethoscope around his neck did the whole thing with torches in the eyes, checks behind the ears and asking pointlessly searching questions. I wasn't so out of it that I couldn't read the notes he made: concussion, post-traumatic amnesia, subconjunctival haemorrhage, fractured ribs and all the other things I could have told him myself if he'd bothered to ask.

In the end he did what they always do: gave me a bottle of paracetamol and told me to come back the next day. I took three of the red and white capsules before I got off the examination couch, then made it to the door under my own steam. Doc was too busy writing up his notes to say goodbye or wish me a speedy recovery, but I knew not to expect any niceties.

As I came round the privacy curtain I could see into the next cubicle. A woman was lying there.

Sleeping, drugged or in a coma? Couldn't tell you. But I can tell you that it was Sanderling.

"Herr Doktor?" I asked the medic, who was still busy with his notes. "The comrade here, will she be OK?"

The doctor glanced up, saw that I was looking at Sanderling and jumped out of his chair. He yanked the curtain shut and shooed me out of the surgery, closing the door behind me.

I leant on the wall of the corridor, wondering about the doctor's reaction. It didn't have to mean anything, I decided. Quite apart from patient confidentiality, the Firm was so obsessed with secrecy that I was sometimes surprised they didn't make us come to work blindfolded.

I headed down the hallway, opening doors as I went. The third door on the left was a bedroom, it looked available: nobody's tat lying around, bed was made. I decided it was good enough for me.

The next morning, the first thing I thought of was a cigarette. Pleased with that—it must have meant I was feeling better, I fished out the pack of Semper cigarettes that Holger had given me, fed one between my lips and lit up.

Bad mistake.

I didn't have anything left to vomit up, but that didn't make it any more pleasant. When I'd finished dry-retching and I'd caught my breath, hand held to my complaining ribs, I looked for the cigarette. It was on the floor, still lit, quietly burning a hole in the brown lino.

I picked it up and pinched it out, then pulled a small rug over the burn mark.

My stomach was still grinding away and my mouth felt like the National People's Army had been testing chemical weapons in there. I needed to sort myself out.

Holger found me in the corridor, trying to remember where the bathroom was.

"Reim—thought you'd escaped again!"

I wasn't in a joking mood, so I left him in the hall and banged into the bathroom, sluicing my mouth out with water before locking myself in a toilet cubicle. But Holger had obviously forgotten his manners.

"You fit enough for breakfast?" he asked through the door.

I didn't bother answering, not verbally. I thought the sound of breaking wind and splashing in the pan would be an adequate response.

"When you've finished here, come and get some breakfast, then we'll have a chat," he continued, his voice echoing around the tiled room.

"A chat? It'll be a bit more than that, won't it?" I flushed and came out of the cubicle, heading for the washbasin. "Who's doing the honours?"

"I am."

I laughed and my head began to spin. A fortnight ago, I'd been asking Holger about the last time he'd seen Bruno, now it was my turn to answer the questions.

41
BUILDING 74
Reim's room

I still had a banging headache, and that little exchange with Holger hadn't helped any, so when I got back to my room, I popped another three paracetamol, swallowing them dry. It was only then that I noticed the fresh suit laid out on the bed. One of my own, Holger must have brought it.

The blue suit from the West had gone, whether to be binned or taken for some kind of forensic examination, I couldn't say. The contents of the suit's pockets were piled on the bedside table, minus the West German identification papers and money. But what I was really after was my hip flask.

I gave it a shake—a drop or two left. I opened the cap and tipped the flask to my lips. The *Doppelkorn* burned as it trickled down my throat, but it straightened my back and sharpened my eyes. I put the flask back on the table, admiring the way my hands were no longer shaking.

After that, climbing into the suit Holger had brought was the work of a minute or two. It was a brown number with light blue pinstripes, bought for me by my wife a few years before she left. The shirt was a lighter brown, another present from the wife, given to me at a different time, one I was also happy to forget.

I didn't feel too bad, despite all the stretching and hopping around on one leg that dressing entails. That counted as progress and I was tempted to try another cigarette to celebrate. But good sense won out and I left the packet where it was on the bedside table, wondering how I'd react to the sight of breakfast.

The sitting room was empty, and the plates of food on the sideboard looked like half of Berlin Centre had marched through, helping themselves to provisions as they went.

I decided to start small, putting a couple of *Filinchen* crispbreads on a plate, a scrape of margarine and a dollop of plum purée on the side.

Sitting at the table, I looked at my breakfast. Usually, I couldn't stand the sight of *Filinchen*, but right now it felt like the right thing to eat. I tried a mouthful, chewing the dry crumbs carefully before swallowing. My stomach growled, but in my book that didn't count as a complaint, so I pasted some marge and plum spread over the top of the next cracker and tried again.

It was one of the best things I've ever tasted, and I wolfed down the rest of the crispbread then sat back, waiting for any late reactions. None came.

It was while I was sitting there, quietly listening to my body, that I realised the paracetamol had kicked in and my headache was now just a dull throb somewhere over the eyes. Perfectly manageable. But now I was no longer concentrating on my head, I was more aware of the bruising that was beginning to show up on my legs and chest. Not pleasant, but nothing I've not had before.

I went back to the buffet, poked the congealed scrambled eggs and felt the cold coffee pot. I left them where they were and took a couple of slices of grey bread, wondering whether to risk any of the cold cuts, but deciding to stick with the plum purée, this time also dabbing some ersatz honey on the side of my plate.

I poured myself a cup of sweet mint tea and took the whole lot back to my table.

"Mint tea? We're not at GST camp," said Holger from the door, implying I was a schoolkid at pre-military training.

"Be nice, I'm a sick man," I grumped into my luke-warm drink.

"Yeah, you're not exactly looking top." Holger sat himself opposite me and watched me cram my breakfast in. "Listen, a heads-up about how this is going to work. I'm to debrief you about your trip to Bonn. As you'll have guessed, the whole thing is a mess and the brass are still arguing about how to share out the blame."

I nodded. I knew better than anyone else just what a mess the Bruno case had turned into, and I had the concussion and the broken ribs to prove it.

"I've never seen it this bad," Holger continued. "If it gets any worse, Mielke's going to have to step in and bang some heads together." General Mielke, the Big Boss of us all, Minister for State Security and, in our imaginations, somewhere on the scale between omniscient, omnipotent god and poison dwarf.

"Who's in the fight?" I asked, wondering whether to get another slice of *Filinchen*.

"Who isn't? Biggest schlamassel ever. My lot in HA II are saying it's their baby since we were meant to be running Bruno and our operatives were the ones keeping tabs on him in Bonn. Your pals in ZAIG are saying they took over co-ordination after Bruno got arrested. If that's not enough, the locals at District Administration Suhl want a slice of the action, even though they know they haven't got a leg to stand on.

"I'm the compromise. I do the first debriefing because I'm already familiar with the case and I'm from II. It's a bit of an olive branch effort."

I sipped my mint tea and thought about Sanderling, asleep or half-dead in the sick bay. It would be nice to know which. "Operative Sanderling, she said she's with your lot? What's she doing here?"

Holger went to the sideboard and poured himself some

coffee. He took a sip and pulled a face, but brought the cup back anyway.

"She was shot. But she'll be OK. She'll stay here until she's in a fit state to be debriefed."

"Shot? Who shot her?" I'd heard only one shot that night on the border. Yesterday—it was only yesterday morning when it had happened yet it felt like a week ago.

"Who shot her?" Holger frowned in warning. "The West Germans shot her. Who else?"

But that shot, I could remember it clearly: it came from somewhere to my left. It came from our side. It wasn't the West German border police who had shot Sanderling.

42
BUILDING 74
Conference room

Holger didn't push me too hard during the debrief, instead he gave me lots of breaks and mint tea. That's not to say he wasn't thorough—he managed to pick up on a few things I hadn't noticed during the mission.

For an hour I described my trip to Bonn and the journey back to the GDR while he sat in silence. He raised his hand when I got to the bit where the Border Scout took me through the gate in the fences, telling me he didn't need to know about that—whatever happened once I'd re-entered the territory of the GDR was out of bounds for the moment.

"Don't want to step on any toes, not until the brass have sorted themselves out," he said. "I'll give you a pen and paper this afternoon so you can write up that part of your statement."

After fetching another cup of sweet mint tea for me, he asked me to repeat the whole story and this time he made notes as we went along. So, once again, I started with the packet of duty-free Marlboro confiscated by the customs officer and ended with the final words from the West German border policeman somewhere in the greenery south of Vacha.

Only the hiss of the reel to reel tape and the creak of the rafters disturbed the silence while Holger read through his notes. We were sitting in some kind of conference room on the top floor of the forestry house, pictures of skiffs and lakes adorned the walls, wickerwork lampshades hung from the collar beams that ran across the roof space. Rustic tables had been pushed together and padded chairs placed around the edge. Holger and I sat at one corner, our cups either side of the microphone that was positioned between us.

"I'm wondering whether the opposition had awareness," said Holger after a short silence, his pen hovering over the part of his notes which covered the train journey. "Someone on the train? Anyone taking an unwarranted interest?"

I thought back to the outward leg of my trip to the West. I'd been vigilant, keeping an eye out, that's just how it is your first time in the operational area—you're nervous, your training kicks in. Plus, I've been getting some practice in spotting and losing tails over the last few months. Still, I'd not noticed anything or anyone on the train.

"Only contact was with an old couple in my compartment. They were from Cottbus, said they were going to a wedding. I didn't regard them as suspicious, although they started to get friendly once we'd crossed the border, so I moved to another carriage when we pulled into Brunswick."

"You felt you had to move?" Holger looked up from his notes.

"Old folk. You know how they are, need someone to blether at so they don't feel so lonely."

"OK. Nothing else? No other contact, no eyes on the train?"

But Holger's pen had already moved on, was now pointing at the paragraph covering my hour's stay in Cologne. "Your dry-cleaning moves before making contact with the informant seem elaborate. Any reason?"

"Caution. My first time in West Germany, wanted to make sure I did things by the book."

"Still rather elaborate," Holger insisted.

I sucked my teeth. What did he want me to say? "I did what I thought was right at the time."

"Any possibles, any hunches that made you go beyond the call?"

"None. It was difficult terrain, so I went the extra mile. No other reason."

"When you made first contact, was there anyone interesting in the bar? Any curious citizens following you down to the boat?"

"It was cold, it was damp. It wasn't the kind of night West German security would be hanging around in doorways—they're too used to comfort for that. Anyway, once on the river, we were out of sight. I told you about the fog."

"And your contacts, the guy in the bar and Sanderling: they used the correct passphrases?"

But Holger knew they had, I'd already told him. He turned the sheet, started reading about Sanderling and my arrival at the empty shopfront in Meckenheim.

"Any contact with Sanderling's observation team?"

"We weren't introduced if that's what you mean. Anyway, I only saw one of them, the other was off shift."

"Of course." Holger pressed his lips together, pulled a folder towards him and flicked through until he settled on a typewritten report. "This is the record of the debriefing of both members of the observation team. Funny thing is, it says here that there was a change of shift while you were in Bruno's flat. So you actually met both of them, didn't you? When you came back from having a look at Bruno, it was a different observer sitting in the shop window."

I thought about it for a bit. Perhaps there had been a change. If that were the case then yes, I should have noticed—it's my job to observe that kind of detail. But I'd been distracted—Bruno's body and all that, not to mention wondering about the other watchers parked in the road.

"You decided to take up operational contact with Subject Bruno. Was that part of the agreed operational plan?"

"Not as such. The operational plan was drawn up on the basis that Bruno would still be in custody. There was zero expectation that he'd be released. Given the change in operational parameters, the difficult nature of seeking further orders from Berlin Centre due to our location in the operational area and the urgency arising from the nature of the development, I decided to exceed the established rules of operational conduct and adjust operational-tactical measures-"

"Yes, OK. I'm just flagging it up. I'd have done the same," Holger interrupted. What the tape didn't pick up were his grimaces every time I said *operational*. He shared my allergy to the O-word—it was used far too often in the formal language of our Ministry.

"The two men in the car on Bruno's street. Any further observations?"

"Sanderling informed me she'd had the plates checked, that it was registered in the name of a local civilian. She suggested the occupants were likely to be members of a West German police agency, possibly Bruno's employer, the Federal Crime Agency. I personally observed that the registration plates were local to Bonn, and the two men were dressed in typical Western clothing."

"Do you agree with the assessment that Sanderling made at the time? Were they police?"

"Age and fitness levels were compatible with active membership of the security organs. But that's, at best, merely indicative."

Holger raised an eyebrow in question, and I nodded: *Yes they looked like police.* Another exchange that didn't make it onto the audio tape.

"I'm gasping for a cigarette," said Holger, even though we could no longer see the decorative fishing nets through the dense cigarette smoke hanging in the air. "Let's have a break."

Holger took me downstairs, gave me a coat and we left the building through the back door. Steps glazed with frost took us past a lifebuoy and a selection of boathooks, down to a jetty at the edge of the Oder-Spree Canal. Ice panned at the banks, but the fairway had been cleared by coal barges coming up from Poland. The wind came from the east, gnawing at our padded jackets. I turned my back on it, but the view was the same. Pine forest broken only by water and the compound behind us.

"Sanderling," Holger began, but paused to blow into his hands. He rubbed them, then stuffed them into the pockets of his jacket. "What can you tell me about her."

I was still facing down the canal, watching the wind push the frozen brash against the sides where it melded with the cracked ice already there. There were no birds in the trees, no fish jumping. The only movement, the only sounds came from the ice, it cracked and moaned, sending shivers of sound through the thin air.

"How is Sanderling?"

"They operated on her arm yesterday afternoon, the doc was talking about some new procedure: osteosynthesis, something like that—they're using screws to hold the bone together."

The cold air hurt my ribs, but I breathed as deeply as I could. "She struck me as a capable operative," I told him, keeping my voice and face neutral. "She did what was needed, and she did it with expertise. Nothing else to report."

"Did you see what happened at the border?"

Holger was lighting a cigarette, and I could feel the pull of it. I wanted to reach over, take it from his fingers, put it to my own lips and breathe in the smoke. But my stomach cramped at the thought of it. I'd have to wait a bit longer.

"Sanderling was some distance away from me, like I told you," I said, knowing he was wondering whether a personal, off the record account would differ from the official version he'd received in the conference room. "She was out of sight when I heard the shot."

"The bullet hit her at the top of the humerus. Went straight through—it's still somewhere in the undergrowth, or embedded in a tree trunk. Either way, it hasn't been found, which makes it difficult to tell whether it came from an Eastern or Western firearm. The G1 rifle used by the BGS has the same calibre as our KM-72, so no help there. Practically all we have to go on is the fact that the entry wound is at the back, she was shot from behind."

"So if she was heading East, towards the gate in the fence ..."

"Then the bullet came from the West," Holger finished the sentence. "A clear case of deliberate provocation by the class-enemy."

There was silence between us for a while, allowing the cracking of the ice, Holger's heavy sucks on his cigarette, the reluctant whisper of the trees in the wind to intrude on our conversation. Holger watched me while he puffed on his nail, his free hand still warm in his jacket pocket.

"Well, now you know the official version. But you may be interested in the report I've seen by the border guard. He was thoroughly debriefed and his account seems credible."

"What does the guard say?" I didn't want to ask, but it was expected of me. My thoughts were on Sanderling, her initial reluctance to come home, how she'd worried she wouldn't fit in, that she'd miss the luxuries of living in the West. Despite all that, she'd been willing to return to the East.

Holger turned to flick his cigarette out over the ice. "Seems Sanderling changed her mind about coming home. When it came down to it, she lost her bottle. Your capable operative Sanderling was shot trying to escape to the West."

43
BUILDING 74
Conference room

We continued the debrief in the conference room. Holger began to ask questions about Sanderling, which made me feel uncomfortable, even though I knew he was merely establishing the facts so he could write up the protocol. The inferences and insinuations would happen further up the chain—whatever had actually happened on the border, the narrative was already being established, and it was obvious to me that Sanderling's career would be over.

"Why did the BGS set off a flare?" asked Holger as I was nearing the end of my account.

"As far as I could tell, it was spontaneous, a response learnt in training," I shrugged. "Incident at border; release flare."

"Could the flare have been set off to guide Sanderling back to the West?"

I had to think about that. Had Sanderling already been shot by then? I wasn't sure. In my memory, the rifle shot and the flare had happened simultaneously. But one thing I was certain about, there had been no contact between Sanderling and the West German border police. There had been no opportunity to get in touch with them before we arrived at the border. And that's what I told Holger.

"The Alouette II helicopter," Holger changed tack. "Did that arrive as a result of the flare, or because of a radio message?"

"I don't know. I was concentrating on the BGS officer standing near me, he was right next to the ditch that marked the border and was talking to me, trying to get me to cross back to the West."

"But he didn't speak to Sanderling?" Holger looked up from his notes long enough to see me shake my head then checked his wristwatch. "Why don't we go for some lunch?"

Lunch, in Holger's book, seemed to start with another cigarette on the banks of the Oder-Spree Canal.

"You want to think about the sequence of events again?" he asked once he'd got his cigarette going.

"Holger, I'm tired. My back aches, my ribs stick into my lungs whenever I breathe in too deeply and my head feels like it's been field-stripped and reassembled in the wrong order. Just tell me what you want."

"The border guard discharged his rifle twice. The first shot was fired into the air as a warning. That happened at approximately the same time the flare was set off. Just before flare goes out, our man fires again. Aims for Sanderling's legs, but somehow hits her below the shoulder. She's on the ground, in shock, and is recovered by a Border Scout who brings her to the Company Headquarters in Vacha." He pulled on his cigarette, giving me a moment to think about what he was saying. "See if you can't remember that second shot, it'd be easier for all of us if you do. That way I'll be able to put it on file and tie a nice, pretty ribbon around the whole thing."

And I did remember. Holger was right that there were two shots. Perhaps. The more I thought about it, the more I tried to picture events in my mind, the murkier it all became. No other word for it: murky. Vague shapes in my memory. Outlines of people moving, no perspective or sense of time.

"Let's get some food, then you can go and see the doc again. But before we go in, I'm going to tell you what to say to the tape machine this afternoon."

★

156

Food was pork goulash in an empty canteen, but I didn't have much appetite. Holger finished off my bowl for me.

"Am I in isolation?" I asked, looking around the empty tables. Holger didn't answer, he was slurping my stew.

I watched him finish the dish then get up for some *Rote Grütze*. He brought me some of the red jelly and I found it easier to swallow than the rich stew.

"Come on," Holger was looking at his watch again. "let's finish off your debrief—I promised the doc I wouldn't keep you too long."

It was a different doctor this time. A big guy, forearms as wide as my thighs. Instead of a white lab coat, he wore a leather butcher's apron over a white shirt and uniform trousers.

"Over here," he ordered, pointing to the examination table with a clipboard.

We did the same stuff as yesterday, torch shining in my eyes, asking me what my birthday was, poking thumbs into my skull to see if there were any soft bits—usual drill.

"Vomiting, tiredness, nausea?" he asked staring at the form on his clipboard.

When I told him I had all of the above, he transferred his attention back to me.

"Problems with memory?"

"Most of yesterday is unclear. A couple of hours are completely gone."

He scrawled something on his form, then asked me whether there was anything else I wanted to complain about. I didn't bother answering. The bruising on my chest and legs, the blood in my eye were all obvious. But the doctor merely stared into the middle distance, tapping the clipboard against his leg.

"Right, follow me."

So I followed him through a door into a smaller room crammed with bulky equipment.

"On that bench, head there." He positioned my head under a heavy piece of machinery, then pressed a button and went behind a screen.

"OK, wait outside," he said after the box of tricks had hummed and clanked a bit. I could hear grinding noises.

I went back into the consultation room and waited on the chair for a moment or two before curiosity got the better of me—time for a short walk around the curtain that divided the surgery in half.

Sanderling was still lying there, attached to tubes and drips. Her eyes were open, but the pupils were slack, she wasn't seeing anything. I picked up the chart hanging at the end of the bed, but didn't understand much, so put it back and went to her side, bending down to take a closer look at her. Her arm and shoulder were hidden beneath some kind of cage that arched over her chest beneath the sheets.

"Sanderling?" I whispered.

The eyes widened a little, the pupils contracting and expanding, trying to get a fix on me.

"You OK?" It's just one of those things you say. You have to ask, even though you know it's a stupid question.

"Dorn?" Sanderling murmured the cover name she knew me by. "HV A watching ... Men in the car. In Bonn, HV A ..."

"What do you-"

"HV A operation, Bru ... Bruno." Sanderling gripped my hand, her eyes trying to focus on my face.

"Comrade!" Behind me, the doctor's voice glinted with displeasure. "I asked you to wait, not to harass the patient!"

He held the curtain open, and I took the hint and went back to my chair. I listened out, trying to work out what the doctor was doing behind the curtain, but no sounds came other than the tap-tap-tap of clipboard against leather apron.

With a rustle of fabric, the doctor appeared again. He marched straight past me and back into the equipment room, where the machine was still grinding away.

44
BUILDING 74
Sick bay

It was another twenty minutes before the doctor appeared again, time enough to ponder over Sanderling's garbled message. The records at the end of her bed said she was on morphine, she must be totally out of it. Anything she said couldn't be treated as credible.

My own mind was bumping along in a low gear, too. Best thing I could do was to wait until I was feeling better, by which time Sanderling should be off the morphine. Perhaps I'd get a chance to talk to her then.

I was busy congratulating myself on my moment of clarity and the resultant plan when the doctor came out of his cubby hole. He had an x-ray with him, and before speaking to me he sat down at his desk, filed the radiograph away in a folder and wrote up a few notes. When he finally turned to me, his swivel chair creaking in protest at the sudden movement.

"You're very lucky, Comrade," he told me. "Plenty of rest, take the paracetamol and seek further advice in a few days if you're still suffering from headaches, nausea or amnesia."

Effectively dismissed, I found my way back to the common area where we'd eaten. Holger was sitting on a brown corduroy couch, reading a stack of carbon copy sheets and smoking.

"The new Stefan Heym manuscript—a good read, but it'll never be published," he said when I came in. "How's the patient?"

"You should know the patient's always the last to be told. The doctor didn't say so in so many words, but I think the prognosis is good. A full life with just a bit of a headache and a hint of a limp."

"That's good news. He told me to go easy on you, can't have you collapsing under interrogation. Anyway, no rush—the brass still haven't got their collective knickers untwisted yet, it'll probably take them a while."

After another brief session in front of the tape recorder, reciting the authorised version of two shots from the East and a flare from the West, I retired to my room, exhausted by the minor exertions of the day. Holger was pleased to be relieved of his babysitting duties and cheerfully gave me a half bottle of vodka and my near-namesake's manuscript to read.

"That'll keep you out of mischief," he smiled. "But don't let anyone see it—you'd land us in trouble."

The lights in the room were bright, but I wrapped a handkerchief around my hand and unscrewed a couple of the hot bulbs, leaving the last one in, it gave off a pleasant glow. I sat in the easy chair, with the sheaf of papers on my lap and by the third sentence I could only agree with Holger that this book would never see the light of day.

The narrative consisted of nothing more than malicious agitation. Heym had composed a deliberately politically divisive text, slandering the great achievements of our state and the unwavering support of the fraternal socialist countries and by doing so, he confirmed himself as a hostile-ideological multiplier.

But the story of how a small part of Thuringia around the town of Schwarzenberg had remained unliberated in 1945—using the opportunity to set up its own Trotskyist structures—was actually quite interesting.

A good read or not, my headache worsened after just ten minutes. For most of the day I'd had a distracting throb between the temples which I'd managed to keep in check with paracetamol, but now it was all about continuous drum rolls behind the forehead. I put the manuscript face-down in a drawer and took a few more tablets.

Then I sat in the half-darkness, my mind returning to Sanderling.

Did morphine make you hallucinate, or just sleepy? How seriously could I take her words? Even if I took what she'd said at face value, she'd only told me that yet another tentacle of our organisation was involved. HV A, the foreign intelligence wing, modelled on the KGB's First Chief Directorate—proudly independent, almost powerful enough to be beyond the reach of the great spider, General Mielke, who sat at the centre of all our webs.

It didn't fill me with joy—in my experience nothing positive ever came from interference by HV A. They could never do wrong, and they used every trick in the Stasi playbook to defend their reputation, no matter what the cost to other departments or the organisation as a whole.

But I wasn't particularly worried, I even closed my eyes and drifted off to sleep. Looking back, benefiting from hindsight, I put my relaxed attitude down to the knock on the head I'd received from the goons down in Saalfeld. I obviously wasn't thinking straight.

45
BUILDING 74
Reim's room

"Reim, are you awake?"

If someone is lying on their bed with their head under the pillow, they're either asleep or want to let everyone know that they wish they were still asleep.

I pulled my head out and tried to glare at Holger, but he was too busy waving a dispatch to pay any attention.

"Word from Major Kühn, I've got the go-ahead to debrief you on your stay in Saalfeld," he announced, waving the flimsy again, just in case I'd missed the significance.

"And that gets you excited because ...?"

But Holger was now in the doorway, waiting for me to get up and to get dressed.

"We could do a quick run-through before breakfast, yes?" he asked, disappearing from sight.

I rubbed my eyes, reached for the bottle of paracetamol and ignored the new shivers of pain that ran the whole way down one leg.

Holger was waiting for me in the conference room on the top floor. He'd thoughtfully brought a cup of mint tea for me, but I reached past it and grabbed his coffee. I took a sip, my stomach didn't complain.

Standing next to the reel to reel, Holger checked I was ready. I gave him the nod and watched as he depressed the record button. A little red bulb flickered into life and the two big wheels began to whirl.

"Yesterday we covered events up to the point when you crossed the border between the West Germany state of Hessen and District Suhl in the German Democratic Republic. Can you now report on events between being brought through the border defences by a Border Scout and arriving here at Building 74."

So I gave it to him. All that I could remember, which was actually more than I'd expected. Things were definitely on the up: I had memory of pretty much everything up until Holger's arrival at the hunting lodge on the edge of Saalfeld. After that, I was a little vague.

We took it slowly, Holger writing notes as I talked. When I'd finished, he stood up, turned off the tape recorder and suggested a cigarette break.

This time I accepted a nail when Holger offered. I took the first inhalation slow and shallow, even though my blood was screaming for a dose of nicotine. I held the smoke in my mouth, waiting for my stomach to revolt, but everything remained calm down there. Another puff. This time holding it in before expelling it into the frigid air.

"This is bloody good," I told Holger, who was grinning again. "Tell me, why so keen to debrief me about Saalfeld?"

"What happened in West Germany, you were just a bystander. You didn't kill Bruno, nor did Sanderling or anyone else on her team." Holger tapped his cigarette, watching the tip flare in the grey light of the winter's morning. "Saalfeld, on the other hand, *somebody* must have thought you were responsible, or at least knew something. *Somebody* was interested in what you did or what you saw around the time of Bruno's death. And that makes me interested in that somebody."

He had a point. Why else had I been held in Saalfeld if not to find out what I knew? "So you're wondering who was responsible for keeping me at the hunting lodge?"

"Aren't you? Don't you want to know why you were being held?" Holger used his cigarette to jab the air between us. "And before you ask: no, I don't know who or why, either. Not yet. I wasn't told when I came to get you and all I know is that your boss and my boss had an argument and then I was sent to find you. Break the speed limit if it got me there faster, your chief said. So that's what I did."

It was colder today, the frost made my eyeballs smart, and I could feel the hairs in my nose turn crinkly. The tips of the fingers of my hand holding the cigarette were cold enough to hurt, but I didn't mind—it helped take my mind off my ribs and the new aches in my left leg.

"Here, look at this." Holger pulled the dispatch from his pocket, the same piece of paper he'd been waving at me first thing this morning. "My orders are to spring this on you later, see how you react. You ask me, the bigwigs have got too much time on their hands. I mean, who thinks up tripe like this?"

I put the cigarette in my mouth and took the flimsy, unfolding it so I could read it. There were just two paragraphs: the first authorised Holger to debrief me on events taking place after approximately 0700 hours on Thursday 29th December 1983; the second paragraph was a basic summary of the test results from the packet of burgers that had been analysed by OTS at the local MfS administration in Gera. Bruno's last meal.

It said the first two burgers in the pack contained over four grammes of thallium salts.

"Thallium? That one of our tricks?" I asked.

"Who knows? Sounds more like something the Friends would get up to. But whoever it was, you were right about Bruno being poisoned."

We smoked our cigarettes in silence while I thought about thallium. I didn't know anything about that poison but going by the state of Bruno's corpse, it wasn't a pretty way to go.

Poor Bruno, he hadn't deserved that.

"I asked the doc, he said it's very hard to trace thallium in the body if you don't know what you're looking for. The symptoms of thallium poisoning match plenty of other conditions which makes it hard to diagnose. Anyway, I'm freezing my legs off out here," said Holger after he'd finished his smoke. He turned to walk the couple of paces back to the door of the forestry house.

"Holger, wait. Thanks for the heads up on that." I nodded at the sheet of paper still in his hand.

"It's in both our interests to get this cleared up." Holger lifted his shoulders in a shrug barely visible inside his padded jacket. "It's only a couple of weeks since you persuaded Kühn that I wasn't responsible for Bruno's arrest. Now it's my turn to make sure you don't get into shit for Bruno being killed on your watch. One hand washes the other."

"Cheers, mate."

Holger had made it sound all very matter of fact, but I was glad it was him doing the debriefing. A less sympathetic interrogator could make the failure of my Bonn mission look deliberate, but Holger was there for me, just like he'd been there for me so often in the past. He'd been a friend even when it had been dangerous to be seen in my company. He'd taken risks when I'd asked him to. Not many people do that, not in our game.

I should treat him better. Not sleeping with his wife would be a good start. Shit, I hadn't thought of Ilona since I'd left for Bonn, now I felt doubly bad. I should tell Holger about what happened, apologise to him.

"Holger," I called to my friend. Perhaps the only friend I had in this life.

"Yeah?" He was opening the door, just about to go into the warmth.

"You got another cigarette for me?"

165

46
BUILDING 74
Conference room

We got back to work in the conference room, tape player recording everything we said. Holger checked minor points here and there for a while before pretending to ambush me with the news about the thallium—I knew it was coming because of the dramatic wink he gave me. I acted surprised for the benefit of the tape, but not too surprised. After all, I'd been at the place of death, had suspected the use of poison in the first place—how much of a surprise could the lab results be?

Holger was grinning like a kid, laughing at Kühn or whichever bigwig had decided that the news of the thallium traces might somehow shock me into revealing something I'd unaccountably been keeping back.

Clumsy, ineffective, but really not a surprise. After all, our whole organisation is built on the premise that everyone is always lying, or at the very least not telling the whole truth.

It was while Holger was winding me up, hamming a serious face that I realised that by taking the packet of burgers, I'd removed the evidence of poisoning. Even if the West Germans worked out how Bruno had died, they wouldn't find the source in his flat.

I didn't care about the West Germans or their investigation, but what Sanderling had told me the previous day suddenly began to make sense.

Who would want to eliminate Bruno that way? For the moment, let's assume it was neither my own department nor

Sanderling's—if ZAIG or HA II had a hand in Bruno's death, they wouldn't have sent me all the way to Bonn to confirm he was a stiff. There were more efficient ways to do that.

Fine, let's rule out HA II, and rule out ZAIG while we're at it. Who's the next suspect on the list? That would be the West German security agencies.

Bear with me for a moment, let's run with the idea that the West Germans knew Bruno had defected. They arrest him as soon as he returns home from visiting his relatives in the East. They interrogate him, confirm their suspicions and decide to get rid of the problem.

Understandably, they didn't want him dying in police custody—that kind of thing gets talked about in the so-called free press they have over there. So they release him and think up a way of killing him at home. That way they can tell everyone it was natural causes, heart attack would sound about right. An easy cover-up.

This wasn't my area of expertise, but if you listen to the rumours that float around Berlin Centre, you'll know the West Germans prefer to avoid obvious wet jobs.

For them, the procedure with suspected defectors is to simply bang them up—four to six years is the going rate.

After the defectors have sat in their cells for long enough, a cosy chat is set up with a tried and trusted go-between, usually the East Berlin lawyer Wolfgang Vogel. A swap is negotiated: Bruno (or whichever defector it may be) is exchanged for one or more of their spies that we've been keeping in storage in Cottbus or Bautzen.

We're better at catching enemy operatives, we have a stash of them in our prisons, ready to exchange a couple for one of our agents of peace who've been careless enough to be caught.

So there you have it, that's our complete list of suspects: two Ministry departments and the West Germans.

Yet none of them quite fit the bill.

You still with me? Then let's consider for a moment that a

third of our departments might have been involved. And this mysterious department would have been the ones who organised my stay in Saalfeld. Sound remotely plausible? If so, then we have another possible suspect in play.

Consider also what Sanderling babbled about an HV A operation and bingo: there's our mysterious third department.

My thoughts were interrupted when Holger tapped me on the arm. I looked up, he was still pulling faces at me, but this time he wasn't trying to make me laugh, his brow was furrowed, his eyes wide, I'd been silent for too long, he wanted me to speak.

"Who did you give the sample to?" he prompted, nodding energetically. "Can you verify the chain of evidence?"

"Er, the sample was in my possession from the time I picked it up in Bruno's apartment until I gave it to the interrogator in Saalfeld. I would have preferred to keep hold of it until I could return to Berlin Centre, but without refrigeration the sample was rapidly degrading. I therefore requested it be passed onto the Operational Technical Sector."

Holger was giving me the thumbs up, he thought my lapse might not sound too bad on the tape.

"My interrogator informed me that he had passed the sample to a member of his team so it could be brought to the District Administration labs in Gera."

Holger gave me another thumbs up and moved on to his next question. He wanted to confirm the name and rank of the beat police officer who had assisted me in Saalfeld, asked me to describe my assailants again, and to explain my reasons for doing them physical damage.

But only part of my mind was on the interview. Most of what was left of my brain was reassessing the Bruno case, seeing whether and how HV A could be added to the mix.

"Are you OK?" Holger asked, frowning again. "You need more painkillers?"

★

I pulled myself together and concentrated on Holger's last few questions. With another smile, he clicked the tape recorder off, noted the time in his notes then, on the way to the door: "Cigarette?".

We stepped outside and Holger shivered. The wind was stronger than before, it stabbed through our padded jackets.

"Come on," I said, carefully picking my way down the steps to the jetty at the edge of the canal.

"You going to tell me what's going on in that head of yours?" Holger asked once he'd caught up with me. He was hunched in his coat, fleece *Bärenvotze* pulled low over his ears.

"I spoke to Sanderling yesterday-"

"Bloody hell, you're meant to be in isolation—you can't just go talking to whoever you want! Why do you think they've got us out here in the greenery? Why do you think the whole place has been practically emptied?"

"Just listen. Sanderling told me the HV A mounted an operation against Bruno."

"And now Bruno's dead?" Holger paused, but not for long: "Sanderling's on the heavy stuff, it's just random words. She's talking gibberish."

"Maybe. But think about it—it all fits: Bruno's dead, and someone took me to Saalfeld. They wanted to squeeze me like a lemon—if I hadn't climbed out the window and called Berlin Centre then I'd still be down there, and they wouldn't be as nice about debriefing me as you are."

Holger didn't answer. He was fumbling for a cigarette, his cold fingers too clumsy to get it out of the packet. I watched him, but didn't help. My fingers were staying right where they were, in my nice warm pockets.

"OK, I'm not agreeing with you," he said when he finally got hold of a cigarette. "But there's something you should see. Last night I was bored: all staff have been withdrawn from the main house and you went to bed early so I had nobody to talk to. I went for a bit of a snoop, managed to find the key to the duty office and had a bit of a look around. Come on, I'll show you what I found."

I followed Holger back up the steps to the forestry house. He didn't bother taking his coat and boots off but headed down the corridor, turning left at the end so we fetched up by the front door. Opposite was a plain internal door, faced in wood effect Sprelacart with a grey, plastic handle.

Holger let me in, shutting the door behind us.

"Here," he said, pulling a folder out of the filing cabinet.

I opened up the file and looked at the top sheet, it was a standard registration form for visitors to conspirational flats. The latest entry was for the 29th of December 1983, the leaving date hadn't been entered yet—that was us. Name of responsible agent was entered as Captain Fritsche, the very same Holger standing in front of me, and the operation was entered as belonging to Holger's department, HA II.

"Look at the previous entries," Holger directed.

So I did. There were about a dozen operations registered for 1983, more in previous years, and every single one was marked with a registration beginning XV.

"Department XV?"

"The local branch of the HV A. And check out the operation at the end of November: that's when I brought Bruno here for preparation to be sent back to the West. See the file registration number?"

"Department XV again."

"Yep. Which is just another way of saying HV A were running Bruno."

"So Sanderling was right? HV A were involved in rubbing Source Bruno out."

47
BUILDING 74
Oder-Spree Canal

"We need to talk to Sanderling," I told Holger. He didn't disagree.

We were back outside. Heavy steel clouds hung low in the sky and the wind tore at every piece of exposed skin it could find. Below us, the canal was almost completely frozen over, even the fairway was covered by a fine skin of ice.

"Tonight," replied Holger, stroking his nose. "At midnight, when the fireworks go off, I'll go and speak to her then."

"Fireworks?"

"You've lost track of time—it's Silvester. Everyone will be out here at midnight, ready to give a warm welcome to 1984."

I had lost track of time. New Year's Eve and here I was in the middle of the forest with my interrogator, a surly doctor in a butcher's apron, several guards and a cook who'd so far done a good job of staying out of sight. But that was fine, never liked New Year's anyway.

"I'll speak to Sanderling, she knows me," I argued, but Holger shook his head.

"Nobody will notice if I disappear for five minutes, but you're different. Everyone's keeping an eye on you."

He was right, still I would have preferred to talk to Sanderling myself. It's all about trust. Given a choice, I wouldn't trust anyone—that's how I've stayed alive all these years.

But hadn't Holger shown himself to be trustworthy? Not

171

just once, but time and again?

Relax, I told myself. *Let someone else do the heavy lifting for a change.*

I was resting on my bed, fully dressed with my boots ready by the door, waiting for Holger.

He knocked on my door at ten to midnight and together we left the building, pulling on our coats at the back door. The staff were already outside, standing at the top of the bank, watching one of the guards set up a battery of fireworks.

It was an awkward gathering—everyone apart from Holger had spent the last few days avoiding me and now we were supposed to celebrate the new year together. The first sentry I'd met when we arrived was kneeling on the ice-hard ground, pulling the foil from bottles of *Rotkäppchen* sparkling wine, ready for the corks to be popped come midnight. The corpulent medical doctor was by my side, minus his leather butcher's apron. He had a Lübzer beer in a gloved hand, and seeing me arrive, reached behind him to take another bottle from a small table set up on the pathway.

"Doctor's orders," he said, handing over the beer. His face was red, perhaps from the wind.

I took the drink and clicked bottles with him. As I sipped the cold beer, I looked around, noticing Holger was helping himself from the table.

"Bit of a tradition we have," the doctor drawled. Seemed alcohol made him collegial. "If we have guests for Silvester, we let off a few fireworks. Give the new year a good start."

Holger nudged me and used his nose to point out an *Unteroffizier* examining his fob watch. "That's the UvD," he whispered. The NCO on duty, the one who should be in his cubby hole next to the main door, making sure nobody tried to have a look at the visitors registration forms.

As I watched, the NCO raised his arm and looked around. "Nearly there, another thirty seconds!" he shouted into the night, and conversation ebbed. The UvD was still looking around, enjoying being the centre of attention. We stood watching him, waiting for the countdown to begin.

"Ten!" he shouted, as Holger began to drift backwards, out of the knot of Ministry goons and towards the door. "Nine!"

Several others joined in, we were all watching the UvD. All except Holger who'd now disappeared inside the forestry house. The countdown continued.

"Four!"

The sentry looking after the fireworks had a long match, was ready to strike it and set off the first rocket.

"Three!"

There was a fizz as the match spurted into brightness. It closed on the fuse just as a deep rumble and clatter of ice lifting and breaking announced the approach of a coal barge, its mast light shining bright between the trees as it came around the curve of the canal.

"Two!"

The doctor reached for a bottle of Sekt, undid the wire cage, ready to knock the cork out.

"One!"

The NCO's final shout was lost in the crack of corks, the shriek of a rocket and a long pull on the ship's horn.

The sentry was already lighting the next fuse, more rockets were shooting up and a pinwheel at the top of the steps to the jetty started whirring around, flinging sparks of light into the gelid darkness.

"*Do siego roku!*" shouted a bargee from the bow of the coal boat as it drew alongside our small celebration.

"*Prosit Neujahr!*" the doctor returned the greeting in German, before mumbling *Fucking Pollacks*, out of the side of his mouth.

But I wasn't listening to the doctor's curses, nor to the barge crew's greetings. As the ship surged past, the helmsman still tugging on the siren, sheets of ice were pushed away from the bows and towards the banks of the canal. In the flicker of the fireworks, and the glare of the red navigation light on the side of the wheelhouse, I could see something in the water.

I scrambled over the bank, out of reach of the sparking pinwheel, slipping downwards until I reached the steps to the jetty. On the slick wooden planks, I knelt down, peering over ice fractured by the passage of boats and healed by freezing temperatures. The barge was past us now, the water slowing and the ice sheet settling back. I turned to grab a boathook and beat the frozen canal.

The metal end of the hook gouged the surface, splinters skidded away. But the body of Sanderling remained trapped underneath. She peered through the frozen water, her dead eyes looking past me, up at the row of Ministry employees at the top of the bank celebrating the start of 1984.

48
BUILDING 74
Reim's room

It didn't take long for the orders to come through. Only a few minutes into the new year but somehow they managed to get hold of somebody senior enough to make decisions. Made me think old Reim was involved in a serious operation and not just a minor housekeeping job.

When I discovered Sanderling's body the goons at the top of the bank moved quickly. I was escorted back to my room and told to wait. Just over five minutes later, Holger was in the doorway, telling me to pack.

I slipped him the Stefan Heym manuscript, then shoved the few clothes I had into the briefcase. It still smelt of rotting meat, but that didn't bother me—I had other worries.

Until this moment, I'd not been too concerned about my own welfare, which may surprise you—after all, those goons in Saalfeld hadn't done my health much good (my ribs thought of them whenever I bent over or climbed the stairs). But the speed with which the evacuation order had come down the line made me rethink my position. Somebody at Berlin Centre was taking this operation very seriously.

By twenty past midnight, I was back in the beige Skoda, heading for Berlin with Holger in the driving seat. I waited until we were on the motorway before I asked any questions.

"Was this eventuality in the operational plan?"

The motorway was practically empty, and Holger had a heavy foot, regularly exceeding the 100 km/h speed limit. He overtook a Trabi puttering along in the slow lane before answering.

"How would I know? I'm not on the operations staff, I'm just following orders, like you."

"Don't you want to know what's happening? Aren't you interested in who killed Sanderling, or how Berlin managed to react so quickly once her body was found?"

Holger took his foot off the pedal as we came up behind a Soviet convoy. He pulled into the second lane and began to cautiously overtake the line of Kamaz trucks.

"When I went to the sick bay, her bed covers were pushed back, you could see where Sanderling had been lying. No sign of a struggle. It looked like she'd just got up and walked out of there."

I thought about that for a moment. Sanderling had been drugged to the eyeballs, in no position to resist anyone trying to take her by force. If ordered to get up and walk to the canal, she probably would have done her best to comply.

"What about me? What are your orders?"

"I'm to take you home and stay with you until told otherwise."

House arrest. Not great, but a step in the right direction. Certainly better than being sent to the Ministry's remand prison in Hohenschönhausen.

We didn't speak again until we were near Berlin. Holger came off the motorway and took the F1 trunk road, bringing us into the city from the east, past the winter quarters of the State Circus.

"My son used to love coming down this road, he'd press his face against the window, hoping to see the elephants," Holger said.

I didn't press my face to the glass, but I did spare a glance at the circus. It looked drab. Lamplit concrete yards between industrial buildings where wagons and vehicles were parked up. No big top, no roller coasters or carousels, none of the sparkle of a circus on tour. No elephants either.

"Did you hear about the time the lads from HA XX went to the circus?" Holger asked. It sounded like the beginning of a joke, but like so much in this country these days, what he said next wasn't funny. "The animal trainers showed them shock and control techniques. If you know how to intimidate a pride of lions then a pack of punks won't cause you any problems."

"Holger, off the record ... I wanted to say ..."

"Yeah, what do you want to tell me?"

"I wanted to say..." I swallowed, looked at the road ahead. To either side was darkness, we were crossing some brook or stream, lots of trees, branches reaching up to the moonlight. "Thanks, Holger."

"Are you being sarcastic?"

"No. You're a good mate, not many of those around. And you've been looking out for me—I know that."

Holger chuckled. "You've changed over the last few months. You're not the Reim I used to know—that tour at a toxic waste dump must have done you some good. But listen, *mate*, you owe me. Big time. And one day, I'm going to call that debt in." He said it in that jokey, half-serious tone we blokes use when we're being open. If he weren't driving he might have patted me on the shoulder. But he hadn't finished yet. "A few weeks ago, I was worried. I don't mind telling you that. When Bruno was arrested, I was shit-scared that I'd run into my own bad case."

The mythical bad case. Except bad cases weren't mythical. We'd all seen colleagues dragged down through no fault of their own. Sometimes it was a silly mistake, more often it was someone else's ambition that saw for them.

"You straightened me out, made sure nothing came of it and I'm happy to return the favour."

And that was the end of it. I'd said what I needed to say and Holger had responded. But there was something else burrowing its way below my ribs, something I needed to let out: "Are you having an affair?"

We were in Mahlsdorf before Holger answered. "Depends who's asking," he said, his jovial tone undermined by the long silence before he answered.

"Bowling practice. Every Wednesday, without fail," I suggested, paraphrasing his wife's words. "Plus all the other times, the evenings when you've had to work late."

"That was you? The night before the big match with your department—it was you, wasn't it?" Holger wasn't asking, he was working it out. "You fucked my wife!"

If you're expecting me to tell you that the Skoda wobbled across the road, skidded on an icy patch and overturned, tragically killing our hero in the moment of his realisation then you'll be disappointed. Holger kept the car under effortless control, but he had to work harder to keep his temper in check.

"How many times?" he demanded. "How often?"

"Just that once. Ilona was frustr-"

"Don't tell me what my wife was feeling!" Holger shouted, slamming his fist into the steering wheel. Finally, the car wobbled a bit, but there was no handy patch of ice to bring the awkward conversation to an end.

"Fuck's sake, Reim! Two minutes ago, we were giving each other declarations of undying love and then you go and spoil it by telling me you've been sleeping with Ilona."

"Just the once-"

"The way you treated your own wife—no surprise Renate decided she'd had enough. So she leaves and you start sniffing around my wife! But best friends, yeah? You couldn't make this shit up!"

I let him rant. Sure, he was upset, who wouldn't be? But he hadn't answered the question, and now I really wanted to know. What does he get up to on Wednesday evenings?

49
BERLIN FRIEDRICHSHAIN

At some point, Holger lapsed into silence and the atmosphere in the car grew so cold that I wound down the window in an attempt to warm up a bit.

Holger dropped me in front of my flat and watched me walk up the path. His instructions had been to stay with me, but he preferred remaining in the car. I didn't invite him up.

Back in my flat, I had a shower then poured myself a drink. Standing in the dark room looking out of the window—the street lights had been fixed while I'd been away—I could see the orange sodium light flare over the roof of the Skoda. I wanted to go to bed, I was beginning to feel a little light-headed, not in the mixing-alcohol-and-pain-killers way, more in a still-broken-after-taking-a-beating way. But first I had some thinking to do.

Delaying the inevitable, I examined my injuries in the mirror. The bruises had come up nicely, plenty of parallel welts from truncheons and a few hoofmarks where I'd been kicked. I pulled on a shirt and sat in my favourite chair, refilled my glass and settled down to work.

Dawn crept through the window and found me fast asleep in my chair. The glass of schnapps had fallen from my hand and was lying on the rug at my feet. I woke with a curse, flexed my head left, then right, trying to crack the ache out of my neck, but it didn't help, so I stood up and stretched. That just made my ribs complain.

From the window, I could see that Holger's Skoda had gone.

In its place there was a Lada the colour of stale blood.

The cupboards in the kitchen were bare, a forgotten packet of *Filinchen* crispbread and a creased packet of KaffeeMix were pretty much all there was, remnants of my wife's last shopping trip before she walked out on me. But I was hungry, so dry crispbread, helped down with the adulterated coffee mix was what I had.

I hadn't managed to do my thinking last night so I had some catching up to do this morning. At this point there were only a few crumbs left on my breakfast plate, and there wasn't much more than that going on in my head.

At the start of all of this, Holger had come to me with a second-hand tale of a mole in the Ministry. he was pretty down at the time, but soon perked up after I'd investigated a little and told him that there was nothing to support the story about a mole, at least not in the material I'd had access to.

But when I looked more closely at Holger's report on babysitting Bruno, I'd uncovered discrepancies. His account of the source's trip home had been full of holes, but that wasn't the only thing that troubled me. I still wanted to know where he went every Wednesday evening—because I was sure he wasn't at bowling practice. His assertion that a Saxon interrogator was the mole was untenable, not least because not a single one of the officers who interrogated Bruno was from Saxony.

Perhaps it's not so surprising that I had questions; look at anyone hard enough and you'll find they're hiding something. Why should Holger be any different? But whenever I'd tried to clear up the inconsistencies, Holger had always avoided giving me clear answers.

Maybe he was in the middle of a nervous breakdown, perhaps he'd been working too hard. It happened, I'd seen colleagues go meschugge many times. First their judgement goes, then they have trouble remembering important things. In the end they're unusable as an operative, kaput, fit only for being hidden away.

I took my plate and cup back into the kitchen and left it by the sink then went to stand in the middle of the living room, between the television and the couch.

Holger had been one of the first to have contact with Bruno, he was likely the only one to have heard Bruno's story about the mole, and he'd been the only one anywhere near Bruno when he was arrested.

Bruno had been well and truly neutralised. After his arrest the Firm wouldn't have trusted anything he said or did, which made his death redundant. So why did he have to die?

And what was Holger's role in all of this? It was possible that he'd caused Bruno's arrest and taken the opportunity to poison the burgers in Bruno's freezer. My friend Holger clearly had the means and the opportunity to eliminate Bruno.

But what about motive?

I sat down on the couch again, picked up the pencil and pulled the pad of paper towards me.

What motive could Holger have had to ensure the Firm would reject Bruno? I could think of only two possibilities.

First up, Holger could have received some kind of reward for neutralising Bruno. But from whom? Just as the Firm has their own means of dealing with inconvenient subjects, Western agencies also have specialised units for that kind of work. No reason to involve Holger—not unless they wanted it to look like we did it. Besides, I've already mentioned that the kind of wet job carried out on Bruno isn't their kind of style. Unless it was some kind of propaganda job? Do the deed and then blame us?

What about the second possible motive? Try this for size: Holger was worried he could be put in danger by something Bruno might say or do. But what would Bruno have on Holger? It would have to be something big.

Both of the above were plausible, at least in the kind of world that Holger, Bruno and I moved in.

So there we have it: motive, means and opportunity—
Holger had all three, and I was sure I could get to the bottom
of it—but only if I was given proper access to Bruno's files. I
needed to see the interrogation transcripts, the evaluations
and analysis reports. The whole works.

I reached for the phone and dialled Kühn's number.

50
BERLIN FRIEDRICHSHAIN

The secretary said she'd call me back, but after half an hour of pacing around my flat the phone still hadn't rung. I crossed to the window, looking down at the cars below. Nobody had left, no new cars had arrived. What do you expect at half-past nine on the first morning of the new year?

But I couldn't stay here, I had an idea in my head—an idea I didn't like—and I needed to prove or disprove it to myself. And if my idea was right? Then I'd lose a friend but I'd keep my job. Probably get a promotion out of it, too.

Whatever. After the ill-judged admission on the journey back to Berlin this morning, I'd probably lost Holger's friendship anyway.

I crossed the room again, but this time I kept going. Through the short vestibule, out of the flat and down the staircase.

The concrete pathway outside was slippery with ice, but I stalked along, wrapping my arms over my chest to ward off the cold. The door of the red Lada opened, and a young man got out. He stood there, watching my approach, one hand on the door, the other holding a portable radio.

"You cold?" I asked and came to a stop a pace or two away.

He didn't answer, his wide blue eyes were fixed on my face, but the fingers of his left hand nervously stroked the transmit button of the radio.

"No need for you to stay out here, you can do your watching just as easily upstairs. I've done the job too many times—I know how it is: freezing your bollocks off, desperate for a piss ... Come on, I'll put the coffee on."

I headed back to the block of flats, turning when I got to the front door and holding it open for the goon still standing in the road. He looked at his radio for a moment or two, then slammed the car door and followed me down the pathway.

"Make yourself comfortable. Toilet's through there, switch the telly on if you like—I'll get the coffee."

The goon hadn't said a word yet, was probably trying to work out how many rules he was breaking by accepting my offer of hospitality. I didn't know what he'd been told at the start of his shift, but I could tell he'd recognised me as a colleague and that had probably swung it for him.

In the kitchen, I turned the percolator on, putting a few teaspoons of KaffeeMix in the filter. Once the water was hissing nicely and starting to bubble through, I left it to do its job and headed to the bathroom.

"Only KaffeeMix, I'm afraid. Run out of real coffee," I told him as I brought the tray into the living room.

The kid was still sitting there, back straight, radio on the coffee table in front of him. He hadn't made himself at home, hadn't put the television on. Was probably having second thoughts about being here.

"Here you go." I poured us both some of the coffee-surrogate blend and watched him pick his cup up.

The young colleague held his drink between both hands, enjoying the warmth. He sipped at it, trying not to grimace. KaffeeMix, what do you expect from a drink that's made from less than fifty percent coffee beans?

He politely finished his cup and, with the exaggerated care of a drunk, put it back on the table, next to his radio. He flopped backwards with a smile on his face.

"Want another one?" I asked.

He didn't answer. He wasn't asleep yet, his eyes were still

open, but his breathing was slow.

"I'm just off out for a bit, you stay here," I told him. "OK to borrow the car keys?"

He tried to answer, but it was too much effort. I dipped into his pocket and took the keys.

I went to the kitchen, emptied my still full cup and the dregs from the coffee pot down the sink, picked up the packet of Radedorm sedatives and put them in my pocket, then put my coat on and left the flat.

I got rid of my wife's left-over sleeping tablets in a bin a couple of streets over, then went back to the Lada and drove myself to Berlin Centre.

51
BERLIN LICHTENBERG

The secretary saw me coming and lifted the phone. A few quiet words, her face set in an even sterner frown than usual, then she replaced the receiver.

"Comrade Second Lieutenant Reim, you are to wait here!" she snapped.

I could have gone straight through the connecting door to Kühn's office, but what I had to report was delicate, I needed to catch my chief in a receptive mood. So I stayed where I was in the ante-room.

There were chairs provided for waiting junior officers, but I was too impatient to sit twiddling my thumbs and looking at the scenery. Whatever Kühn was up to in there, it wouldn't take long—it was New Year's day, how full could his diary be?

But it did take a while. Under the liverish gaze of the secretary, I soon ceased my pacing and sat on one of the chairs reserved for the likes of me. I watched the wallpaper for a while then I stared at the portrait of General Mielke, so familiar I could draw it from memory. I looked out of the window at the static blanket of cloud that wouldn't shift for another three months. But waiting for a superior is like doing sentry duty. You straighten the back, point the eyes forward and switch off higher cognitive functions.

And just like sentry duty, you have to be able to snap to attention in less time than it takes for a door to open.

When I saw grey uniforms through the doorway, I stood up, eyes straight ahead, waiting for whoever it was to pass through my field of vision on their way out.

Comrade Major General Koschack, head of section IX of the HV A and Comrade Lieutenant-Colonel Schur who headed up HA II/2, Holger's department.

Major Kühn had been in conference with the big fish, and that on New Year's day. Something was brewing.

"Reim!" the order, such as it was, came from Kühn. He didn't bother with the honorific comrade-plus-rank—I was in trouble.

I followed him into his office, closing the door behind me. He was already sitting down, and I came to attention the regulation number of paces before his desk.

"Make this good," he ordered, leaning over his blotter, hands clasped in front of him.

"Comrade Major, regarding the case of Source Bruno. Here at Berlin Centre, I have detected the activities of a hostile provocateur-"

"Watch your language!" Kühn rasped.

That threw me. Watch my language? We were talking about the possibility that Holger might be working for the other side, was maybe even a long-term mole, a double-agent who had burrowed deep into the Ministry ...

"We all know HV A prefer to keep to themselves. Their actions may have been borderline provocative, and I accept that you haven't been treated well by them, nevertheless I forbid you to refer to our distinguished colleagues in the foreign intelligence department as hostile provocateurs!" Why was Kühn blethering on about HV A?

Sanderling's last words to me had been about the watchers in Bonn being from HV A, that they'd been running an operation against Bruno. And now Major General Koschack of HV A had just walked out of this very office. *When in doubt, shut up*, I told myself.

And it was good advice, Kühn assumed I was keeping my gob shut out of respect, not confusion.

"How did you work it out?" he asked.

I risked a quick glance downwards, far enough to see whether or not the question was genuine. Kühn seemed interested, this time it wasn't one of those rhetorical questions that superior officers like to leave lying around the place for us juniors to stumble over.

"The watchers in the locally registered vehicle outside Bruno's place of residence, Comrade Major." I risked another flick of the eyes downwards to gauge the major's reaction. He was wrinkling his nose, which made his eyes creep even further under his beetle brow.

"Didn't see that in any of the transcripts of your debrief, Comrade Second Lieutenant," he announced, like a judge reading from a prepared sentencing statement. "Care to explain?"

"In the absence of firm proof, I thought it prudent to reserve my statement until I could make a personal and informal report, Comrade Major."

"Which is why you're here. Next time, go through the proper channels, Comrade." It sounded like a dismissal, but then the major started up again. "Of course it's nothing to do with us, but if I were in charge of HA II, I'd be referring the matter to the Minister's office. Inserting First Lieutenant Gerhard Sachse into an HA II operation wasn't in the spirit of political-operative co-operation-"

"*Der Sachse, der war es ...*" The words popped out when I heard Kühn mention the name. *The Saxon, it was him.*

"First Lieutenant Sachse has returned to his post at HV A." My interruption irritated the major but he decided to ignore it. "And I've just had the heads of both departments in here. I smoothed things out a little, but if HV A had concerns about Source Bruno they should have gone through the proper channels."

"Permission to speak?" I asked. If the major was feeling expansive, I wanted to make use of the opportunity, fill in a few more gaps. "I wish to report suspicions regarding Bruno's research into the West German terrorist organisation the Red Army Fraction and his presence at Building 74, commonly used by the HV A." I was extrapolating on the few facts I had.

"Building 74 is regularly used for housing and training RAF operatives. HV A wanted to make Bruno available so ex-RAF members now resident in the GDR could confirm or deny that he was a danger to activities in the operational area. Bruno was recognised by said operatives, and based on the analysis that his offer to defect was part of a hostile-negative operation to undermine operative co-operation between the HV A and active members of the RAF, HV A took the decision to neutralise him."

I was still processing the news that HV A had eliminated Bruno when another thought intruded. When you're standing at attention, staring at the wall above a superior officer's head, you don't have much brain-space to spare. Sure, you might think standing there gawping at the wallpaper shouldn't require much in the way of thinking capacity, but let me tell you, you need to stay alert. Superiors like nothing more than to trip you up—it's like an interrogation, you never know when they're going to slip something into the conversation, make you say something you shouldn't. It's not called standing at attention for nothing.

And the thought that intruded on my standing around? Holger.

If HV A were the bad guys in this one, if they'd decided to liquidate Bruno, then there was no mole.

Holger wasn't the mole. I'd suspected him, which made me not just a pillock, but a poor friend. Again.

"Anyway," said the major. "Not our concern. I want a full report from you next week, in the meantime, aren't you meant to be on sick leave?"

"Comrade Major!"

Clickety-heels. Exit.

52
BERLIN WEISSENSEE

The condensation on the cold windscreen was crystallising, with every exhalation I added further clouds of moisture. My hands were red, my fingers numb.

I could run the engine, switch the heater back on, get warm and drive home and see how the young goon was doing, whether the sleeping pills had worn off yet.

Or, I could get out of this icebox, cross the car park and ring Holger's doorbell.

With a sigh, I opened the car door and got out. I pushed the door shut and locked up, the whole time watching the windows of Holger's flat. A light was on—it was the middle of the day, but the cloud layer was so dense and low that it felt like dusk.

I walked across the car park, wondering what I'd say to Holger. *Sorry* didn't quite do the job. I could say: *Sorry, old friend—I suspected you were a mole, but it's all OK because I didn't get a chance to denounce you to the chief.*

I gave the front door a push, it clicked open, so I headed up the stairs to Holger's flat. I could hear music through the door, something synthetic and poppy, not my style. And the shouting was even less to my taste.

The door was ajar, so I went in.

"Holger, please!" Ilona had pasted herself against the living room door at the end of the hall. She was on her knees, her fists banging the wood.

I ran towards her, passing a teenager standing there, mouth hanging open, wonky glasses. That'd be Hannes. Nice kid in a not-so-nice situation.

I was next to Ilona by now, trying to pull her upright.

"What's going on? Ilona, tell me!"

She was still sobbing and shouting, I slapped her.

That got her attention. She turned away from the door long enough to slap me back, then carried on banging her fists against the wood, shouting for her husband.

Her wedding ring had caught one of the bruises on the side of my face, opening it up. I could feel blood trickling down my chin. I took a step back, wiped the blood away and assessed the situation. Ilona wasn't going to let me distract her, so I decided to join in.

"Holger!" I banged on the door. "It's Reim—let me in!"

And he did. The key clicked in the lock, and I shoved the door open.

"I'll deal with this," I told Ilona, holding her back as she tried to follow me into the living room.

I managed to shut the door on her and turned the key again. Only then did I turn around and look at Holger. He was standing by the window, looking at the cars parked below, a Makarov pistol in his right hand.

"I was watching you down there in your car. Wondered how long it would take you to work up the courage," he said to the glass.

I stayed where I was, back against the door, I could feel it shudder as Ilona's fists continued their pounding.

"You come to apologise or to arrest me?" The glass misted where his breath hit it. Holger turned around, slowly, as if I was the one holding the gun.

But all I had were words, and precious few of those. We looked at each other, I tried to read his gaze, hoping his eyes would tell me why he was in a locked room with his service weapon drawn.

"Holger, the Bruno case is all wrapped up. We know everything."

"I've been waiting for you." He waggled the pistol in his right hand. "Now you're here you should sit down."

He gestured at an armchair, the one I'd sat on the night I was here for dinner. The one Ilona and I had fucked on.

"I panicked when Bruno started talking about a mole, knew my time was up."

"Holger?" He really was meschugge.

"Shut up, Reim! You've come to get me, fine. But let me tell it my own way." He turned back to the window again, wiped the condensation away with his left sleeve.

I could rush him, seize the Makarov. But he was already turning around again, whatever he wanted to say, he wanted to say it to my face.

"It was me. There you are, that's the word straight from the mole's mouth." He wiped his sleeve across his nose, the pistol passing in front of his eyes. "I've been waiting for a long time for Bruno to activate me. We had a legend prepared, you want to hear it? I was meant to become his handler, but actually *he* was my handler—clever, isn't it?" Another wipe of the sleeve, Holger was crying. "We don't give the West Germans nearly enough credit—they come up with a plan like that, years in the making—they deserve some credit."

He grinned at me. Not a grin like yesterday at House 74, it wasn't friendly or warm. It was without meaning

"So why did you tell me there was a mole?" I asked, eyeing his *Wamme*. "It doesn't make sense."

"I needed to test my legend. You and I, Reim, we've known each other since we both started out—if you couldn't see what was going on then I knew I'd be safe."

"And if I exposed you?"

Holger raised the pistol, pointed it at me and made an almost silent *peng* noise with his lips.

"You got away with it," I told him, trying to keep my voice level. "Nobody knows. Just us two."

"You hear that?" he gestured at the door with his left hand, the one not holding the gun. Ilona had stopped banging, was no longer shouting, but her sobbing still plucked the air. "*They* know, there's no going back from this." He still had the Makarov trained on me. "And *you* know, too. So *peng.*"

"Why was Bruno arrested?"

"HV A. They suspected something, I needed to throw them off. So I sent a message to the West: arrest Bruno. But it didn't help, HV A got to him anyway. And now they've sent you—that's a step up for you, working for Mischa Wolf's boys. It's all over. Too late." He raised his right hand, and took aim at me.

"Wait! There's still a way, I think I can still get you out of this ... I came to tell you how we can ... we can ..." I didn't recognise Holger, his eyes were dark, the empty grin pasted to his face was as wide and hard as a lion's. "Triple agent! We play you back to the West but the Firm is in control—they'll like that, they'll boast about it to the big brothers in Moscow. You'll get a medal!"

I leaned forward in the chair excited by what I was saying. Holger was still pointing his grin at me, and the gun didn't look any less dangerous. I could rush him, nothing to lose—go on Reim, get yourself out of that chair and disarm him!

"There's no future for me here. Look after Hannes and Ilona for me—you'll like that, won't you, an instant family?" Holger edged back until he bumped up against the window again, out of reach.

Perhaps he wasn't going to kill me—can't expect me to look after his wife and son if I'm dead, can he? But I didn't relax, not yet. Holger was too unpredictable.

"You heading West? You got a plan? You know what they're like, they'll track you down, they'll kill you or bring you back —they never give up." I was gabbling, trying to buy time, enough time to work out how to disarm him.

"The problem with you, Reim ..." The arm holding the Makarov was shaking, the finger behind the trigger guard was trembling. "The problem with Comrade Reim is that people like the idea of him more than they actually like him."

Before I could answer, Holger's forearm jerked back. In one swift movement, the muzzle of the pistol went under his chin and his finger tightened on the trigger.

When Ilona broke the door down, she found her husband's body on the carpet and the back of his head spread over the window.

EPILOGUE

There were three funerals in January 1984.

I heard that Bruno was buried with full honours in Osnabrück, West Germany, his family and colleagues at the graveside.

Over here, in East Berlin, I attended the Baumschulenweg cemetery in my dress uniform. We stood there in the cold, a dozen comrades from the Ministry on one side of the hole in the ground, Lieutenant-Colonel Schur standing at the head of the grave, mouthing socialist platitudes to the gusting wind.

Ilona and Hannes didn't listen to the officer's empty words, and they did their best not to look at Holger's old colleagues. Ilona had an arm around her son, but the wetness on her cheeks was rain, not tears. Hannes didn't cry either, he clasped his hands, as if in prayer, and watched as the four NCOs slowly paid out the ropes, letting Holger's coffin sink into the grave while we officers shivered.

I hadn't reported my last conversation with Holger. There was no point, it would only have unleashed the wolves and I couldn't afford that level of scrutiny.

I hadn't spoken to Ilona since New Year's Day, we hadn't exchanged a word since I'd held her next to the body of her husband. I'd told her what to do, what to say, then I'd phoned an ambulance and instructed them to take the body to the Institute of Forensic Medicine in Hannoversche Strasse.

After the ambulance had gone, I returned to Berlin Centre and informed Holger's colleagues of his death, telling them that I'd been concerned about his mental health ever since I'd interviewed him a couple of weeks earlier.

The coffin bumped against the bottom of the grave and the

ropes were pulled out. Ilona released a handful of damp earth over the hole then turned away, pulling Hannes with her. She strode down the path, making no attempt to avoid the puddles and mud. She ignored the car the Ministry had provided and passed through the cemetery entrance.

Around me, Holger's ex-colleagues began to relax. Hands and heads were shaken, kind words were spoken. The lieutenant-colonel was already being ushered into his Chaika by the chauffeur.

"You were with him when he died?" one of the colleagues asked me, a captain.

I didn't answer. I was still watching Ilona's receding back.

"Had a bright future, did Comrade Captain Fritsch. What a waste ..." The captain's words were as empty as those of the lieutenant-colonel.

I waited until I was the only one left. The gravediggers were nowhere to be seen, they'd be in their cabin, drinking beer and waiting for the rain to ease. I looked down. Holger in his grave, handfuls of mud and a tangle of red chrysanthemums on top of his coffin.

"Goodbye old friend," I said. "I'm sorry."

The crematorium worker and I were the only ones present. He had the oven door open, the white tiles on the walls and floor flickered and shone in the light of the flames.

In the middle of the room, a plain wooden box was mounted on a trolley. I watched from the side as the worker took a form, placed it on the top of the coffin and signed it. He folded the paperwork and put it in his pocket then wheeled the trolley forward. With a jolt, the coffin slid over the lip of the furnace and into the flames.

The heavy oven door closed, and the worker went off, leaving me alone with Sanderling's burning body. I still didn't know why she'd been shot, whether it was true that she'd changed her mind and was trying to escape back to the West.

But I had connections, in time I'd find out.

"Goodbye Sanderling," I said. "We could have been friends."

I walked out of the crematorium and between the graves, heading for the gates. And maybe those were tears on my cheeks, not rain.

I thought about what Holger had said to me the day he died, the last friendly conversation we'd had.

You're not the Reim I used to know.

The East Berlin Series

'An authentic atmosphere of tension and uncertainty ... The brilliance of *Stealing the Future* lies in the honest portrayal of a young country and its idealistic inhabitants struggling to keep alive their dream of freedom, justice and equality in the face of international and domestic opposition.'

Jo Lateu, *New Internationalist*

'A compelling re-imagining of East Germany's peaceful revolution in 1989—exploring what might have been. As Europe grapples with the consequences of austerity, this novel poses questions both about the lost chances of 1989, and about how we organise our society—questions that are more relevant with each passing day.'

Fiona Rintoul, author of *The Leipzig Affair*

'An intriguing and gripping page-turner of a thriller—believable and exciting. More than that, though, it's an exploration of power—political, economic and electric power; and what it might be like, day to day, to put our ideals and hopes for self-determination into practice.'

Clare Cochrane, *Peace News*

Printed in Great Britain
by Amazon